PUFFIN BOOKS

PONGWIFFY AND THE SPELL OF THE YEAR

Apart from writing children's books, Kaye Umansky has been a drama teacher, a television presenter for educational programmes and has also sung in a band! She is married with one daughter and lives in London.

PONGWIFFY
a witch of dirty habits
and the
Spell of the Year

KAYE UMANSKY

ILLUSTRATED BY CHRIS SMEDLEY

PUFFIN BOOKS

PUFFIN BOOKS

Published by the Penguin Group
Penguin Books Ltd, 27 Wrights Lane, London w8 5tz, England
Penguin Books USA Inc., 375 Hudson Street, New York, New York 10014, USA
Penguin Books Australia Ltd, Ringwood, Victoria, Australia
Penguin Books Canada Ltd, 10 Alcorn Avenue, Toronto, Ontario, Canada m4v 3b2
Penguin Books (NZ) Ltd, 182–190 Wairau Road, Auckland 10, New Zealand

Penguin Books Ltd, Registered Offices: Harmondsworth, Middlesex, England

First published by Viking 1992
Published in Puffin Books 1993
1 3 5 7 9 10 8 6 4 2

CONTENTS

The Cast   viii

Map   x

CHAPTER ONE
An Interesting Find   1

CHAPTER TWO
The Spell   11

CHAPTER THREE
Dunfer Malpractiss   20

CHAPTER FOUR
Ye Wilde Cat's Whisker   26

CHAPTER FIVE
Ye Quicksande   35

CHAPTER SIX
Ye Vulture's Feathere (Barry Gets His)   46

CHAPTER SEVEN
Ye Locke of Goldene Hayre　　　51

CHAPTER EIGHT
Rumblings　　　62

CHAPTER NINE
The Twins Come Calling　　　70

CHAPTER TEN
The Demon Barber　　　78

CHAPTER ELEVEN
Ye Bobble Off Ye Hat of a Gobline　　　87

CHAPTER TWELVE
Banned　　　94

CHAPTER THIRTEEN
Ronald　　　108

CHAPTER FOURTEEN
Tea at Sharky's　　　117

CHAPTER FIFTEEN
Seven Stolen Stars   131

CHAPTER SIXTEEN
Brewing Up!   144

CHAPTER SEVENTEEN
Ronald Tells   154

CHAPTER EIGHTEEN
Caught in the Act   158

CHAPTER NINETEEN
Spell of the Year   171

CHAPTER TWENTY
An Encounter at the Bar   185

CHAPTER TWENTY-ONE
Wishing Water   196

CHAPTER TWENTY-TWO
A Lovely Surprise   204

ALSO FEATURING: The Goblins
AND INTRODUCING
Princess Honeydimple
&
Ronald (the Magnificent)
☆ ☆ ☆

SPECIAL FLEETING GUEST APPEARANCES
The Spiders, the Toad, Demon Barber, Clifford the Troll, Brenda the Zombie, Frank the Foreteller.

MASTER OF CEREMONIES
Ali Pali

ESTEEMED JUDGING PANEL
Sourmuddle, Harold the Hoodwinker, Scott Sinister, Dunfer Malpractiss, Pierre de Gingerbeard, King Futtout, Fumbling Phil and his Feathered Friends.

PLUS THE USUAL HANGERS ON
Banshees, Skeletons, Wizards, Spooks, Odd Gnome, Thing in Moonmad T-Shirt, etc.

PRODUCED BY
KAYE UMANSKY
GRAPHICS
CHRIS SMEDLEY

CHAPTER ONE
AN INTERESTING FIND

'Well now, just look at this! Hey, Hugo, look what I've found!' called Witch Pongwiffy from the murky depths of an ancient chest.

At the time, they were in the middle of spring-cleaning – yes, *spring-cleaning* – Number One, Dump Edge, which is the name of Pongwiffy's hovel. Well, if you want to be strictly accurate, Hugo and the Broom were spring-cleaning and Pongwiffy was getting in the way.

'Oh my. Now vat she got? Old bird's nest? Anuzzer overdue library book?' sighed Hugo to the Broom, who was wildly rooting about under the kitchen table.

The Broom gave a disinterested shrug. It had never been allowed to sweep up before, and was terribly over-excited. It had just built its first ever pile of dirt, and right now all it could think about was adding to it.

'No, really!' insisted Pongwiffy. 'This is really interesting! Come on down and see for yourself.'

'Nein. I spring-cleanink,' said Hugo firmly.

He was standing on the top step of a rickety step-ladder, swiping at cobwebs with a feather duster. He had declared war on the Spiders, and nothing was going to stop him.

'Spring-cleaning my foot! I'm talking *Magic* here. Look at this! It might well be the discovery of the century!'

Pongwiffy emerged red-faced from the chest and scuttled across the hovel, scattering the Broom's beautiful dirt-pile in all directions. In her hand, she held a large, mouldering book.

'Look! Granny Malodour's old spell book! I've often wondered where it got to. She gave it to me for my eighty-first birthday. Of course, I was just a youngster then. Thought it was old-fashioned sort of stuff, never really bothered to look at it. And it's been at the bottom of the chest all these years. Oh, stop it, Broom!'

The Broom was enthusiastically trying to sweep her out the door. Being so new to this spring-cleaning business, it hadn't quite got the hang of things yet. Pongwiffy gave it a brisk kick which sent it zooming off into a sordid corner where it worked away humming to itself, not being the type to bear a grudge.

'Well, well, well. Just fancy. Old Granny Malodour. It's ages since I thought of her.'

'Who Granny Malodour?' asked Hugo.

'You've never heard me talk of Granny Malodour? If you think *I'm* smelly, you should have got a whiff of Granny. Lived by herself in an underground cave. Shared it with a skunk for a while, but even he had to come up for air eventually. She was an expert on cave fungus, you know. There were at least six varieties growing on her sofa. And as for Magic! There was no one to touch her. She kept at it, you see, down in that old cave of hers. She only came up for important family gatherings. When there was

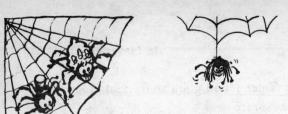

cake. She was a Serious Witch.
You wouldn't catch her wasting time
doing stupid *spring-cleaning*!'
Pongwiffy glared scornfully at
Hugo, who shrugged and continued with his
dusting.

'I'll never forget her famous Wishing Water,'
continued Pongwiffy nostalgically. 'Wonderful stuff,
that was. She used to send up a bottle every Hallowe'en, I remember, and we'd all get a sip, even us
little kids. Tasted disgusting, but it was worth it.'

'Vy? Vat 'appen?' asked Hugo, curious despite
himself.

'Why, we'd all get a wish, of course. And it
always came true. Granny's potions were like that.
Very reliable.'

'Vat you vish for?' asked Hugo.

'A little Sweet House all of my own,' said Pongwiffy dreamily.

'Vat 'appen to it?'

'It melted in the heat and flies got stuck to it. In
the end I had to throw it away. But it was lovely
when it was new. I can taste that chocolate guttering
now.'

'Vishing Vater sound good stuff,' said Hugo. 'Vy ve not make some?'

'I wish we could,' said Pongwiffy regretfully. 'Granny Malodour always kept the recipe a secret. Mean old thing. Probably thought it wasn't good for us to get too much of a good thing. Oh, do stop flicking that duster about, Hugo, you're driving me mad. Leave the stupid old spring-cleaning. So what if there's a crumb or two on the floor? I couldn't care less.'

'That because you not 'Amster,' Hugo pointed out. 'Me, I live close to ze ground. It hell down zere.'

It was true. For anyone under six inches, the hovel floor was a minefield. If the toast crumbs didn't get you, the smelly socks would. If by some miracle you avoided both, the chances were you'd slip and drown in a puddle of skunk stew.

But if it was bad at ground level, it was even worse higher up – because higher up were the Spiders.

Ooh, those cocky Spiders. They were

really getting above themselves these days, acting as though the place belonged to them. Just recently, they'd taken to practising daredevil trapeze acts on the trailing cobwebs which looped from the ceiling.

'Hoop-la!' they yelled to each other in Spider language. 'OK, Stan, now the triple roll, after three! Don't worry, I'll catch yer!'

Hugo had put up with it all for as long as was Hamsterly possible. But when high diving into his bedside glass of water became the latest Spider craze, he had dug his paws in and declared that Pongwiffy must choose between him and the dirt, for one of them had to go.

After careful thought, Pongwiffy had decided to part with the dirt. After all, dirt could be replaced, whereas a good Familiar was hard to find. Besides, he owed her eleven pence.

'You're supposed to be my Familiar, remember?' Pongwiffy reminded him, picking bits of cobweb from her mouth. 'I do think you could show a bit more interest. After all, it is a family heirloom.'

Crossly, she opened the ancient cover and gave a wail of disappointment.

'Oh no! The bookworms have been at it. Look, they've chewed up nearly every page!'

'Typical,' said Hugo. 'All zat fuss about nussink. Typical.'

'Oh, wait a minute! There's something written on

the inside of the cover. It looks like Granny Malodour's writing. It's faded, but I think I can make it
out. Where are my reading glasses?'

'Zem I sling out.'

'You threw out my *reading glasses*? How dare
you!'

Pongwiffy was outraged.

'Zey got no glass. Zey not glasses, zey frameses,'
Hugo pointed out.

'I know, but that's beside the point. I always saw
better with them.'

Huffily, Pongwiffy carried the disintegrating book
to a window so that she could see better. Hugo was
still concentrating on cobwebs and hadn't got to the
window-cleaning stage yet. The cracked pane was
so encrusted with dirt that it let in marginally less
light than the wall. Pongwiffy briefly considered
cleaning it, then smashed it with a poker to save
time.

Hugo made a remark in Hamsterese that sounded
worth translating. The Broom did a double take at
the sound of falling glass and came rushing up, keen
as mustard. The sun, long a stranger to the inside of
Pongwiffy's hovel, came bursting in curiously,
lighting first on the opened book with Granny
Malodour's spidery writing scrawled mysteriously
all over the inside cover.

'Well I never did! Would you believe it! Just

fancy that. Hugo, guess what Granny's written inside the cover!'

''Ow I know?' said Hugo with a shrug. 'Vat?'

'The recipe! The *recipe*, Hugo! For Wishing Water! Oh, this is the most amazing piece of luck! Just think, Hugo, Granny's secret recipe, and it's been passed down to me! Ooh, I simply can't wait to try it out. You don't get spells like this nowadays, Hugo. There are some very interesting ingredients. It'll be quite a challenge getting hold of some of these, I can tell you. Oh yes, quite a few raised eyebrows. Hey! I've just had a thought! I could enter it for the Spell of the Year Competition!'

'Ze vat?' asked Hugo.

'Spell of the Year Competition. As advertised in the *Daily Miracle*. The winner gets a big silver cup, and all sorts of super prizes. Where's yesterday's paper?'

'I sling out. I sling out all ze papers.'

'You threw it *out*? Idiot!'

Furiously, Pongwiffy ran out of the hovel. There was a scrabbling noise, followed by the sort of slithering crash that might be made by a very tall pile of old newspapers falling from a very great height. Then she was back.

'Found it. Look!'

Eagerly, she waved the *Daily Miracle* under Hugo's nose. Hugo looked. Sure enough, the Spell of the Year Competition took up most of the front page.

'Vat make you sink ve vin?' said Hugo.

'Win? Of course we'll win. What chance has a common old Cure For Warts or a stupid old Frog Transformation Spell against a bottle of Granny Malodour's Wishing Water? I tell you, Hugo, with a superior spell like this, we can't fail. Anyway, it's time a Witch won for a change. Last year it was won by some stupid old Magician with pigeons up his jumper. Batty Bob and his Boring Birds or some-such. We'll have to keep it terribly secret, of course, I don't want the other Witches knowing. If they know I've got Granny's recipe, they'll all want it.

We'll have to work undercover. Ooh, I simply can't *wait* to get started, can you?'

'Ja,' said Hugo firmly. 'I can. Right now, I do spring-cleanink. You vanna do Magic? Get your vand and mend zat broken vindow.'

'I shall do no such thing,' said Pongwiffy. She snatched up her wand, threw it in a chair and sat on it, sulking. Hugo and the Broom ignored her, and quite right too.

CHAPTER TWO
THE SPELL

Late that night, sitting in her rocking-chair, in a spanking-clean hovel, nose buried in a hanky, Pong-wiffy brooded over Granny Malodour's spell.

All was quiet. Hugo had flaked out on top of a pile of ironing. His cheek pouches sagged with exhaustion and he was snoring loudly.

Outside the hovel, the Broom was soaking its

sore bristles in a bucket of water. At the foot of the pail, a multitude of evicted Spiders were preparing for the long trek to the promised land with bitter little cries of, 'Come on, boys, we know when we're not wanted,' 'Don't forget the flies, Gerald, we'll be peckish later,' and things like that.

Pongwiffy peered at the ancient writing by the light of a single candle. She couldn't stand it any brighter in the hovel, because everywhere was so blindingly clean it hurt her eyes.

She hated it. She loathed the way the pots and pans glittered and the way the floor winked at her, daring her to walk on it in muddy boots. She liked her cardigans how they were before, all comfortably matted up and dirty brown with those special holes for her elbows. Pink and blue they were now, with a sissy smell that came from something that Hugo poured in the water.

In fact, everything smelt all wrong, even the air, which Hugo had sprayed with something out of a can called Reeka Reeka Roses. The only way she could breathe was with a hanky over her nose. The hovel just didn't feel like home any more. Pongwiffy

hardly dared move without the Broom following her about in case she dropped a crumb. And Oh! the fuss Hugo had made when she attempted to climb into bed without washing her feet.

'Oi! Vat zis you do?'

'I'm going to bed, if you must know.'

'Not vizzout vashink ze foots.'

'Wash my *feet*? *Me*? Have you gone *mad*? Why?'

'Cos zose is clean sheets.'

'Uggh! So they are!'

Pongwiffy jumped away from the bed as if scalded. 'You don't expect me to sleep in *those*, do you? They're – they're *white*! Yuck, I nearly touched one. Where are my old grey ones?'

'Zem I sling out.'

'*You threw out my sheets?*'

'Ja. Zey not nice. Zey got 'oles. Zey got crumbs. Zey like bottom of ze birdcage.'

'I know. It took years to get them like that, you interfering Hamster. Well, if you think I'm getting in between *those*, you can think again. I'd sooner stay up all night.'

'OK,' said Hugo yawning. 'Me, I go sleep.'

So that's why we find Pongwiffy in her rocking-chair in the small hours of the morning, brooding over Granny Malodour's spell.

And this is what it said:

Wishing Water
(YE RECIPE)

- 1 × Whisker of Wilde Cat

- ½ × Bucket of Beste Quicksande

- 1 × Feathere of Volture

Freshe Locke of Goldene Hayre from Ye Hede of A Pryncess (Pref. Cut at Midnight Under Fulle Moone.)

1 × Bobble off Ye Hat of A Gobline

Seven Stolen Stars from A Wizard's Cloake of Darknesse

½ × Pint Skunke Stocke

12 oz BEETLE DooZ

FROGSPAWNE & FLY DROPPings to Taste

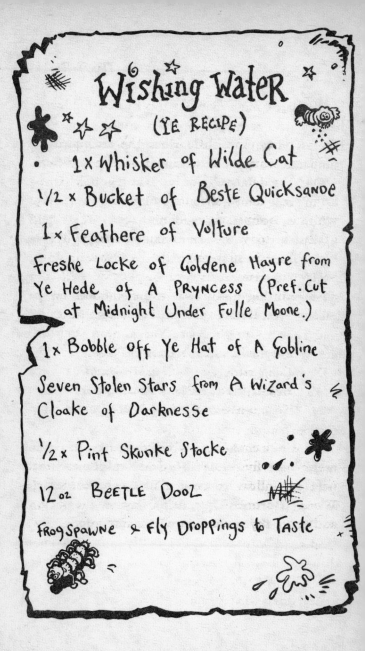

Method

On ye night of ye fulle moone, place ye quick-sande to simmere in cauldron over a low fyre. Using thy left hand only, take thou a sharpe knyfe and finely chop dry ingredients (hayre, whisker, bobble, feathere and stars). Mix. Add gradually to ye hot quicksande, stirring all ye time. Pour in skunke stocke. Add beetle doos. Season to taste. Bring to boyle. Sit with thy nose pointing due north and thy boots on ye wrong feet. Recite thou ye following chant:

> *Snap and crackle, scream and cackle,*
> *Can't catch cows with fishing-tackle.*
> *Bubble, brew, the way thou oughter,*
> *Then turn into Wishing Water!*

Continue chanting until thou hearest ye cockerel crowe five times. Remove cauldron from heat and allow to cool. Then say ye Magick Words (Bottoms Up!), drink thou of the potion and make thy wish. Best with a side salade.

'Hmm. Sounds easy enough,' muttered Pongwiffy. 'Mind you, some of these ingredients could
be a bit tricky. Best have a look to see what I've
got.'

Candle in hand, she marched to her Magic cupboard. Now, usually her Magic cupboard was stuffed
so full that the doors exploded outwards the moment
they were touched. Jars of frog's-legs, packets of
beetle-eggs, old wands, cracked crystal balls and
paper bags of mysterious powders marked DOTE
NO WOT THIS IS would all come tumbling out
in a huge, satisfying jumble.

Not now, though. Now it was empty. Hugo was

nothing if not
thorough.
'Right,' said
Pongwiffy grimly,
surveying the bare
shelves. 'Time to make
a list and go shopping,
I think.'
The next half an hour
involved the back of an
old envelope, the stub of
an old pencil, a great
deal of head-scratching
and a fair amount

of scribbling. As soon as the list was finished, she seized her basket and rammed her hat on.

'I'M OFF, THEN,' she announced in an unnecessarily loud voice. 'OFF TO THE SHOPS. STOCKING UP.'

She needn't have bothered. Hugo merely snored even louder. Scowling, she kicked the door open with an almighty crash and stomped out into the moonlit night.

Outside the hovel, the Broom slept in its bucket. All around the front garden, tall piles of beloved junk teetered under the moon, doomed to be returned to the rubbish tip the following morning.

There was her favourite battered old sofa, the one that had nearly got stolen by two mummies last Hallowe'en. And, oh no! there was her photograph album with those irreplaceable snaps of Witch Gaga being sick at last year's Coven outing to Sludgehaven-on-Sea!

Ah! There was her framed letter from Scott Sinister, the famous film star! And there, scattered about all over the place, lay her collection of rude notes to the milkman, which went back seven years. And, oh no! there were her oldest, smelliest, comfiest cardigans, the ones which Hugo considered a health hazard and refused to wash. There was her first tall hat, a bit battered to be sure, but bringing back fond memories. And there was her box of old wands and her first chemistry set and a pile of crumbling books with titles like *Know your Omens and Portents* and *My First Little Book of Curses*. And there was her favourite hot-water bottle, and her dead poison plant and her second worst cauldron . . .

Pongwiffy's eyes misted over. But not before she became aware of the accusing stares of a hundred or more exiled Spiders, who muttered and pointed resentfully.

'Huh. Some landlady.'

'After all we done for her.'

'Never got behind with the rent, did we, Mother?'

'Oh, Dad! Never to dangle from me own little rafter again. Webless, at my age.'

'Never you mind, Ma, we'll look after you. We'll find you a little nook where you'll be made welcome, see if we don't. Right, boys?'

'I don't think me poor old legs'll get me there. I got terrible rheumatism in all eight knees. Anyway, it won't be home. I'll die of a broken heart, I know I will. If somebody don't step on me first. Or a bird don't get me.'

All of this made Pongwiffy feel even worse. With a guilty flush and a heavy heart, she slunk away, heading for the Magic Shop. A shopping trip might take her mind off things.

SNIFF
SNIFF

CHAPTER THREE

''Ear yer bin spring cleanin' dahn your place,' remarked the man behind the counter with an unpleasant leer. His name was Dunfer Malpractiss and he was the owner of Malpractiss Magic Inc., where all the Witches went to buy ingredients for their spells.

Malpractiss Magic Inc. was, as is usually the case with these sort of places, a wandering shop which came and went as it pleased. You could never be absolutely sure, if you ran out of eye of newt on a Saturday night, that Malpractiss Magic Inc. would even be around to sell you any, let alone have it in stock.

However, Dunfer Malpractiss wasn't stupid. He had a lot of regular customers in Witchway Wood, and the likelihood

DUNFER'S NEW INTRODUCTORY OFFER REEKA REEKA ROSES

was that Malpractiss Magic Inc. would be found in the usual place (by the stream under the old oak tree) most nights between the traditional opening hours of midnight and dawn.

'None of your business what I've been doing,' snarled Pongwiffy.

'Yer. Not before time, I reckon. Always was a bit of a tip, your place,' mused Dunfer, sucking his moustache. It was one of those unpleasant wet ones which droop into cups of coffee and always get covered in froth.

'So? I like it like that. Are you serving or what?'

'Keep yer 'air on, keep yer 'air on. What were it you wanted again?'

'I've told you!' Irritably, Pongwiffy waved her shopping list under his nose. 'I need a Wilde Cat's Whisker, some Beste Quicksande, a Vulture's Feathere, a . . .'

''Old on, 'old on. One fing at a time. Wilde Cat's Whisker, were it?'

'Yes.'

Dunfer Malpractiss pulled at his nose with dirty fingers.

'Nah. Fresh out orrum. What were the next?'

'Quicksande.'

'Nah. No call fer it these days. There's a pool of it in the wood somewhere, go an' 'elp yerself.'

'What about Seven Stolen Stars from a Wizard's Cloake of Darknesse?'

'Nah.'

'A Bobble off ye Hat of a Gobline?'

'Nah. Old-fashioned sort o' ingredients, ain't they? What sorta spell you doin', anyway?'

'Never you mind. What about Beetle Doos?'

'Nah. No call.'

'Skunke Stocke cubes?'

'Nah.'

'Frog-spawne and Fly-droppings?'

'Nah.'

'Well, you're not much help, I must say,' grumbled Pongwiffy. 'I suppose you haven't got a Vulture's Feathere either?'

'Nah. Gorra coupla budgie ones goin' cheap.'

'Certainly not. It says Vulture, very definitely. I don't know, I thought this was supposed to be a Magic shop. What *do* you sell here?'

She glared around crossly. The shop was full of shelves, and the shelves were full of jars, bottles, cans and boxes. Several sullen-looking used broomsticks slunk around behind the counter. That was funny. Why weren't they in their usual place? Pongwiffy suddenly noticed that the used-broom rack was stacked with brand-new, bright-yellow squeezy mops with white plastic handles.

'Cleanin' stuff, mostly. Spring-
cleanin' time o' year, ain't it? Yer, I got soap 'n'
mop-'eads 'n' tins o' beeswax 'n' air-freshener in cans.
Want some? Reeka Reeka Roses, this year's smell,
very popular, on special offer, I'll do you a squirt . . .'

'Don't you dare!' cried Pongwiffy in alarm. 'Now
look, Malpractiss, I'm not *interested* in your cleaning
stuff. I'm a Witch, remember, and what I'm interested in is Magic. Got that? So what I want is
quicksand and a bobble and a whisker and a feather
and a fresh lock of hair from the head of a Princess,
and if you can't help me, I'll just have to . . .'

''Ang abaht, 'ang abaht. A lock o' golden 'air orf
a Princess's 'ead, did yer say?'

'Yes. Why, have you got one? Strictly speaking,
it should have been cut at full moon.'

'Fink I kin 'elp you there, matter o' fak. Now,
where were it again . . .?'

Slurping into his moustache, Dunfer Malpractiss disappeared into the gloomy shadows at the back of the shop. Moments later, he returned.

'There yer go!' he announced triumphantly, slapping down a dusty old shoebox on the counter. 'One lock o' golden 'air, guaranteed orf a genuine Princess's noddle. That'll be twelve pahnd . . .'

'Just a moment,' interrupted Pongwiffy, taking the lid off the box and peering suspiciously within. 'Is this fresh? The recipe distinctly calls for fresh.'

'Eh? Oh yer, fresh as anythin', that,' said Dunfer, looking shifty.

'Then how come it's grey? This is *grey* golden hair.'

'Eh? Nah, trick o' the light . . .'

'Trick of the light my foot. Look at the sell-by date on this box, you old fraud. See? BEST USED BEFORE THE STONE AGE.'

'Yer? No kiddin'? 'Ang on, less 'ave a dekko . . .'

'Never mind. I shall take my custom elsewhere in future,' said Pongwiffy grimly, and strode out with her empty basket.

'Sure yer don't want no bin-liners?' came the sad cry.

'Only to stick your head in,' retorted Pongwiffy rudely, and set off through the trees. Disappointment had made her all the more determined. All right, so

Malpractiss Magic Inc. had been a complete waste of time – but the night was yet young, and there was more than one way to skin a cat.

Thinking of cats reminded her of the first ingredient of Granny Malodour's spell. A Wilde Cat's Whisker.

The nearest thing Pongwiffy knew to a wild cat was Deadeye Dudley, the battered, one-eyed tom-cat who belonged to Witch Sharkadder (Pongwiffy's best friend. Sometimes). In fact, they didn't come any wilder than Dudley, who had spent one of his nine lives as ship's cat on a pirate ship. Or so he said.

'I'll go and ask Sharkadder right now,' declared Pongwiffy, setting off through the trees. 'The direct approach usually works. After all, she is my best friend.'

But first, she decided to pop home and collect a few of those rock-cakes she had made last month. Just as a little gift.

She hoped Hugo hadn't slung them away.

CHAPTER FOUR

YE WILDE CAT'S WHISKER

'Oh, it's you,' said Sharkadder, opening the door a grudging crack. 'What do you want, Pong? I'm terribly busy. I've just finished washing my floor. I don't want your dirty great boots all over it.'

Pongwiffy was shocked. 'Washing the *floor*? What, *now*? But it's the witching hour! Why aren't you cackling over a brew?'

'Because I'm spring-cleaning. It was lovely to see you, Pong. Now go away. Come back in the morning.'

'But I've brought you some rock-cakes. Fresh

baked this afternoon,' lied Pongwiffy, trying to force her basket of month-old rock-cakes through the crack.

'Oh, really?' said Sharkadder, immediately suspicious. 'What for? What d'you want?'

'Nothing. Why are you so suspicious all the time? Oh, come on, open up, Sharky. I thought we were best friends. I've had an awful evening. I've just been to the Magic shop and couldn't get a thing I wanted. I just want to put my feet up for two minutes and have a glance at your catalogue. Let me in, do.'

'Oh, very well,' sighed Sharkadder, suddenly taking her shoulder away from the door. Pongwiffy fell past her into the cottage. 'But you're not to stay long. I haven't started the polishing yet.'

Sharkadder waved a tin of beeswax at Pongwiffy and tapped her foot impatiently. She wore a frilly apron with little green frogs embroidered on the pocket. A matching green scarf was twined around her head. Her precious talons were protected by rubber gloves.

Pongwiffy stared around in disapproval. Everything twinkled and gleamed back at her.

'Looks nice, doesn't it?' said Sharkadder.

'No,' said Pongwiffy. 'What's that awful smell? Wait, don't tell me. Reeka Reeka Roses. This year's smell. On special offer.'

'How did you know?' said Sharkadder, impressed.

'Never mind. By the way, what are you doing for this year's Spell of the Year Competition?'

'Oh, I don't know. I'll probably enter the formula for my new spot cream. Why?'

'Oh, nothing. Here are your rock-cakes,' continued Pongwiffy, holding out the basket. 'I tried out a new recipe. Same as the old one, but you add the granite chippings *after* the egg. That's why they might be a teensy bit harder than usual.'

'Oh, lovely. Very kind. I'll get the hammer,' said Sharkadder, who knew Pongwiffy's rock-cakes of old.

'Oh, don't bother now. I should save them until after I've gone,' said Pongwiffy hastily. 'Otherwise you might get chippings all over your nice clean floor.'

'As if you cared about that!' cried Sharkadder. 'Although,' she added curiously, 'correct me if I'm wrong, a little bat told me you've been doing a bit of spring-cleaning yourself!'

'Not me,' denied Pongwiffy stoutly. '*They* are. Hugo and the Broom. Not me. I don't approve. I like my dirt.'

'Nobody else does, though, do they?' Sharkadder pointed out. 'I bet I'm the only visitor you ever get at your hovel.'

'No you're not,' protested Pongwiffy. 'Loads of visitors come to Dump Edge.'

'Don't shout, Dudley's asleep. Anyway, they

don't. Nobody ever goes there because it's so disgust-ingly dirty and smelly. Even Sludgegooey said she thought you ought to clear up a bit more, and you know what *her* place is like. Actually, talking about visitors and you being so dirty and smelly and everything reminds me: whatever happens, *do not* come to tea next Sunday.'

'Oh. Why not?' asked Pongwiffy, crestfallen. She enjoyed going to Sunday tea with Sharkadder. There were snail and cucumber sandwiches and sometimes little bat-shaped biscuits with currant eyes, as well as one of Sharkadder's delicious fungus sponges.

'Because my nephew Ronald is coming, that's why.'

'Oh,' said Pongwiffy. 'I'm not good enough for your relations, then?'

'Exactly. He's just passed his Wizard exams, you know. With honours.'

'I know,' said Pongwiffy. 'You told me.' She had little time for Wizards in general. For Ronald she had no time at all.

'Did I? He's done awfully well, you know. He's a member of the Wizards' Club now. It's very exclus-ive. There's a password and everything. All terribly hush-hush. Well, it would have to be, wouldn't it? I mean, you don't want any old riff-raff wander-ing in. Ronald's going to have his own chair and everything. They're going to give him his very own locker to keep his wand and sandwiches in. And his own peg in the cloakroom. Did I tell you?'

'Yes,' said Pongwiffy. 'Several times.'

'Oh yes, he's done quite brilliantly,' boasted Sharkadder. 'Top of his year, he tells me. He's rather hoping to become a Royal Wizard, you know. Straight in at the top.'

'He would,' said Pongwiffy.

'Yes, he's got an interview with King Futtout over at the Palace the day after tomorrow. I've bought him a lovely Good Luck card with horseshoes on it. Do you want to sign it?'

'No,' said Pongwiffy.

'I'm sending him some of my new skin cream to try and do something about his spots. Oh yes, he's got my brains all right. A pity he hasn't got my complexion. Anyway, he's coming to tea on Sunday, and I don't want you here letting me down.'

'Oh, but . . .'

'No. That's final. I want everything to be nice. Ronald's used to nice things. At the Wizards' Club they eat off matching plates, you know. With paper serviettes and everything. He told me. I'm not having you here smelling the place up and putting your boots on the table and making rude remarks. Understand?'

'I suppose so,' sulked Pongwiffy.

'Good. That's settled, then. Here – you can take the catalogue home to look at if you like. If there's nothing else, goodbye.'

'Actually, old friend,' said Pongwiffy, 'there *is* something. I wanted to ask you a small favour.'

'Oh, you did, did you? Now we're getting somewhere. What?'

'I was just wondering if you could spare me one of Dudley's whiskers, actually.'

'Oh, you were, were you? Why?'

'Oh, you know, no special reason.'

'I suppose you need it for some stupid spell. Well, even if he agreed, which he won't, how do you propose pulling it out without hurting him? He's got feelings, you know. He's not a machine. You can't stick a coin in him and wait for a whisker to drop out.'

Pongwiffy hadn't thought of that. Uneasily, she peered into Dudley's basket. He was spitting and hissing and flexing his claws in his sleep, heavily involved in one of those fierce, piratical dreams of his.

'Well, I suppose the easiest thing would be to give him a little tap on the head with a mallet or something. That way he wouldn't feel a thing.' Pongwiffy didn't feel too hopeful as she said it.

'How dare you,' said
Sharkadder coldly.
'I'll tell him you
said that when he
wakes up. He'll probably
scratch you.'
'No he won't. He's too
scared of Hugo. Oh, come on,
Sharky, it's only a *little* favour . . .'

'Yes, that's all you ever want, little favours! Well, I'm tired of doing you favours. Go and pull out a whisker from that pint-sized Hamster of yours. You think he's so wonderful, don't you? Just because he beat up my Dudley once. Well, let me tell you, Dudley had a bad back at the time. He's still got it, as a matter of fact. If he was in good health he could make hamsterburger of your Hugo, so there.'

'Oh no he couldn't,' said Pongwiffy stoutly.

'Oh yes he could,' insisted Sharkadder, hands on hips.

'No he couldn't.'

'Yes he could.'

'Couldn't.'

'Could.'

'Couldn't.'

'*Could*. Wake up, Duddles, darling. Silly old

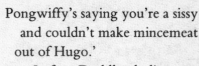

Pongwiffy's saying you're a sissy and couldn't make mincemeat out of Hugo.'

In fact, Duddles darling was really awake, but didn't want to get involved. He still had the scars from the last time he had tangled with Hugo. That Hamster was *tough*.

'I'd help ye haul that barrel, shipmate, but I got this bad back,' he muttered, pretending he was still dreaming. He didn't fool Pongwiffy.

'There, see? He's a scaredy-cat. He's afraid of my little Hugo, I told you so.'

'That does it! Out! Out of my house this minute!' ordered Sharkadder.

'I take it I don't get the whisker, then?'

'You certainly do not. The cheek of it.'

'That's the last time I bake you rock-cakes.'

'Good! This is what I think of your rock-cakes.'

Sharkadder threw one on the floor and stamped on it. The heel came off her shoe. The rock-cake remained intact.

'Right!' said Pongwiffy, hurt. 'That does it! I'm breaking friends.'

And she picked up her basket and marched out, breaking into a run as rock-cakes whizzed past her head.

It seemed that the direct approach had been all wrong.

As she walked up the path to her spotless, un-friendly hovel, the Broom leapt to attention and proceeded to fussily sweep the path behind her. She put her hand on the door, and a bossy squeak commanded her to wipe her feet.

She paused, sniffed, smelt the unmistakeable smell of Reeka Reeka Roses and decided to sleep under the stars on that old mattress in the rubbish tip. Spring-cleaning indeed!

CHAPTER FIVE

YE QUICKSANDE

The next morning, Pong-
wiffy rose at daybreak. She did
some deep, healthy breathing by the
compost heap then, holding a hanky
over her nose, crept into her
hovel where Hugo and the
Broom still slept. Moments
later she marched
out again with a bucket
and a large soup ladle.
Determinedly she set off
down the path, soon leaving
it and plunging

deep into the trees, heading towards the quicksand.

Very few people visited the quicksand. It wasn't that much of an attraction really, consisting of a still, treacherous stretch of stagnant water where only worms, snakes and oozy things lived. Even the trees seemed darker and more sinister in this neck of the woods.

However, it took more than a vague air of brooding menace to stop Pongwiffy. Bucket in hand, she barged through brambles and clumps of stinging-nettles, lips clenched in a thin, white, determined line. Finally, she burst from the thicket into a small clearing, noticing just in time that the ground was spongy beneath her feet.

Very, very slowly, she inched forward. Her boots sank deep into the bubbling sludge and came up again with sucking slurps. They were two sizes too big and without laces, so Pongwiffy had the greatest difficulty keeping them on.

Balancing with great care on a tiny clump of marsh grass, she stooped, wobbled a bit, readied her bucket, and dipped her spoon in the quicksand.

Now then. Here's an interesting turn-up. Pongwiffy didn't know that this quicksand was, in fact, the home of a certain Toad. A Toad who once (and not that long before either) had spent the best part of an unforgettable Saturday evening up to his neck in batter, destined to be the main ingredient of Pongwiffy's toad-in-the-hole supper.

Pongwiffy didn't remember this. But the Toad did.

There he was, enjoying a quiet snooze on a slimy rock, getting away from the wife and tadpoles for ten precious minutes, when out of the bushes burst the Raving Lunatic who had sprinkled him with chopped parsley that time before, sticking him in a dish of grey goo and donging him with a spoon every time he popped up for air.

The Toad remembered her all right.

The Toad noted with pleasure that the Raving Lunatic had a rather nasty bramble scratch down one arm.

He observed with glee that the Raving Lunatic had recently fallen over and banged her knee and ripped some enormous holes in her cardigan.

He was also pleased to see that the Raving Lunatic was edging towards the quicksand, stooping, wobbling, very insecure, definitely a bit nervous.

He wasn't that interested in the bucket – a rusty, battered old thing – but *he was very interested in the spoon*!

Slowly she stooped, slowly – slowly – and the Toad waited, nearly dying with pent-up giggles, the sort you get when playing hide-and-seek and the

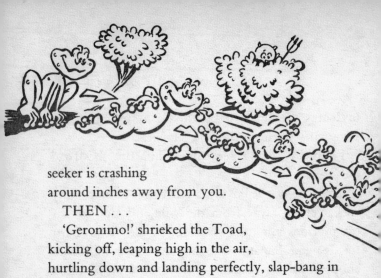

seeker is crashing
around inches away from you.

THEN...

'Geronimo!' shrieked the Toad,
kicking off, leaping high in the air,
hurtling down and landing perfectly, slap-bang in
the middle of Pongwiffy's bony shoulder-blades.

'AHHHHH!' howled Pongwiffy, arms whirling
like windmills as she strove to keep her balance.

The arm-whirling didn't work, of course. Neither
did the frantic grabbing of the nearest thing, which
happened to be a blade of marsh grass. It did its best,
but Pongwiffy was just that bit too heavy and the
marsh grass wasn't built for it. It snapped, and Pongwiffy pitched forward, shot out of her boots, did a
clumsy somersault, and entered the quicksand head
first. The bucket fell out of her hand and landed
some feet away, vanishing with a slurping glug.

The spoon, however, was saved from a similar
fate by the Toad, who, with a triumphant cry of
'HOWZAT!' caught it deftly by the handle as it
arced through the air. A malignant grin on its face,
the Toad then waited for Pongwiffy's head to
surface. As soon as it did, the Toad gave a flying leap,

landed on it and proceeded to batter it with the spoon.

'Dong!' croaked the Toad, bashing away with malice. 'Dong, dong, dong! There. How do *you* like it?'

'Hey! What the – look, get *off*, will you? Stop *doing* that, you crazy animal. I'll sue you for assault and battery, I'll . . .'

Booble groggle burble . . .

(That's supposed to be a Sinking-in-quicksand sort of noise. Perhaps you can do better?)

'Don't give me batter,' snarled the Toad, very worked up indeed. 'I'll give *you* batter.

Now, get back down there. Dong, dong, DONG!'

It could have been nasty, couldn't it? We could have lost our poor old Pong then and there. She could have sunk without trace, the victim of a blood-crazed Toad armed with a soup ladle.

We didn't, though. Help was at hand, in the form of none other than Witch Macabre's Haggis Familiar, whose name was Rory.

Now, you should know that Haggises are odd-looking creatures with a great deal of shaggy fur, two sharp horns and daft-looking ginger fringes, which hang in their eyes. They are grazing animals,

normally content to spend all their time chewing
cud and mooing at passers-by. Occasionally, however, they like to enjoy what they refer to as a Wee
Wallow, and are happy to have this wallow in
quagmire, marsh, swamp or bog. Best of all, though,
they like quicksand.

That very morning, as luck would have it, Rory
felt bored. He was left very much to his own
devices during the day. (Macabre was one of those
sensible Witches who sleep from daybreak to sunset,
unlike Pongwiffy who, day or night, can always be
found rampaging about being a nuisance, which is
why she gets overtired and ratty sometimes.)

After chewing cud for an hour or two and swag-
gering around his field showing off to tiny birds and
harmless moles, Rory decided it was a good day for
a Wee Wallow. Pausing only to collect his towel, he
set off, tail flicking and horns held high, skittishly
trampling pretty little clumps of daisies with his
thumping great hoofs and snorting at dainty butterflies. (Well, I don't know what you expect, I'm
sure. That is correct behaviour for a Haggis, particularly one who happens to be a Witch Familiar.)

He was aiming, of course, for the quicksand. It
was his favourite Wallow Spot. It was always nice
and quiet there, and he could float around for hours
practising his backstroke without people saying, 'Oh,

ha, ha. Look at that stupid Haggis doing backstroke, what a show-off, who does he think he is?' and so on.

Emerging from the bushes, Rory was very put out to find what he thought of as his own private pool already occupied! Somebody was already floundering around enjoying themselves in the thick mud, and Rory didn't like it. Particularly as that somebody looked suspiciously like Pongwiffy, who isn't the sort of person you'd care to share a bath with. Her filthy old boots were sitting forlornly on a clump of marsh grass, but apart from that she appeared to be fully dressed, with the exception of her hat. She was doing a lot of arm-waving and thrashing about, obviously having a wonderful time.

'Och, ha, ha, ha, will ye look at yon Witch doing the backstroke, wha' a show-off, who does she think she is?' remarked Rory in a loud, sneering way, hoping that his taunt might put her off her stroke and make her go away. Nothing of the kind. In fact, she floundered around more vigorously than ever.

'Och, ha, ha, ha . . .' began Rory again, thinking she hadn't heard, 'will ye look at yon Witch doing the ba –'

Then he broke off, for Pongwiffy appeared to be howling something at him.

'What?' returned Rory. 'Ah'll no lend ye ma toowel, if that's what ye want . . .'

'No, you idiot! Get – me – OUT of here, quick, I'm . . . groogle bobble blurgle . . .'

She was what? Groogle bobble blurgle?

Rory shook the fringe out of his eyes and looked again. On closer inspection, it appeared that Pongwiffy wasn't enjoying herself at all. In fact, she was having a rather horrible time. Possibly something to do with the fact that there was a demented-looking Toad battering her head with a wooden spoon, saying, 'Dong! Dong! Take that! Dong, dong, DONG!'

'Help me, Rory,' bawled Pongwiffy.

'Dong! Dong, dong, dong, dong, DONG!'

Groogle bobble blurgle . . .

At long last, Rory got the message. With a heroic moo, he reared, pawed the air with his hoofs, then charged to the rescue.

The Toad gave a startled croak, dropped the spoon and leapt for the bank, just as Rory landed with a titanic squelching splosh in the quicksand. He looked for the bubbles which indicated where Pongwiffy had foundered, dipped his head under the surface, hooked his horn into the back of her cardigan and yanked her up.

She emerged with a plop, spluttering and gasping, saved in the nick of time. Which just goes to show that Haggises have got what it takes in an emergency. Even if they haven't at other times.

Triumphantly, Rory waded to firmer ground with his exhausted, squelchy burden dangling from his horn. To say that Pongwiffy was relieved would be an understatement. She had swallowed so much mud that her insides were like Sludgehaven-on-Sea at low tide. Her head ached from the spoon-battering it had received, and at one point her cardigan had ridden up most uncomfortably. Nevertheless, she still had enough energy to swear vengeance on the Toad, who had returned to its slimy rock and sat watching the rescue operation with sulky, defeated eyes.

It was an embarrassing episode – but it had a happy ending. Pongwiffy did what she set out to do. She got some quicksand. In fact, later that day, she squeezed enough of the beastly stuff out of her rags to fill a bath-tub. She made a nice mess of the floor in the process too – but Hugo and the Broom were very efficient and cleaned up after her in no time at all. This was a shame, as for five minutes, there, with all the little puddles and trails of muddy footprints, her hovel had almost looked like home again.

CHAPTER SIX

YE VULTURE'S FEATHERE (Barry Gets His)

Witch Scrofula lived in a dark, tacky little cave on the west side of Witchway Wood. She lived with her Familiar, a vulture called Barry. Barry suffered from an embarrassing Personal Problem. It had to do with feathers – or, rather, the lack of them.

You see, a year ago he had commenced moulting. This, as everyone knows, is the natural process whereby birds shed their old feathers in order to grow a new batch. Barry had managed the first bit of the process beautifully, losing all his feathers virtually overnight apart from a few fluffy ones growing in a scruffy ruff around his scrawny neck. However, it was now a WHOLE YEAR LATER, and he was still waiting for the new ones to grow. It was most upsetting. People were calling him Baldy instead of Barry. Besides, he was permanently chilly.

Poor Barry. Far from being a sight to strike terror into every heart, he was now a figure of fun. He had tried everything – exercise, a balanced diet, vitamins, beakfulls of quill pills, wing massage, aromatherapy – but none of them worked. He tried combing the sad, wispy little neck feathers every way, growing them long and plastering them over his naked back with grease – but they just looked pathetic and fooled no one.

Just recently, however, hope had grown in the shape of a large, glorious, glossy tail-feather. There was only the one, but it was a start, and Barry spent long hours preening it and admiring it with the help of a complicated system of mirrors. He almost dreaded going to sleep these days in case it fell out, but – on the other hand – maybe when he woke up another one might have grown, so there were two ways of looking at it.

This particular morning, Scrofula was in her cave, washing her hair. Scrofula washed her hair several times a day, being martyr to a virulent and alarmingly stubborn form of dandruff. Even at the height of August it always snowed on Scrofula's shoulders. It was odd, really, them both suffering from the same sort of ailment.

Barry was outside, dozing nudely on a low branch after a heavy lunch of garlic pills washed down with hair-restorer. He was dreaming. In his dream, he was the owner of gloriously luxuriant plumage. It

was the sort of plumage that had parrots nudging each other and peacocks turning green with envy. In his dream, everyone kept asking him for preening tips and telling him he ought to be in westerns.

Little did he know, the poor bald thing, that a certain Witch was at this very moment stealthily reaching up towards his rear end, evil intent writ large upon her face and a sharp pair of shears in her hand.

The first he knew about it was being rudely woken by a piercing scream, and he opened his eyes to see his mistress bearing down upon him with a towel round her head and a look of utter horror on her face.

I don't think we'll stay to hear any more, do you? It's just too sad.

★

That night, Pongwiffy proudly showed the feather to Hugo.

'There,' she said. 'One Vulture's Feathere. And I've got Ye Quicksande, of course. That makes two things already. A pity about Ye Wilde Cat's Whisker. Of course, if only you'd stop being such a disgusting little house-Hamster and give me a hand, I'd get on a lot quicker. It's funny, you know, Hugo. When I took you on, I never thought you'd neglect your duties as a Familiar. Ah well, only goes to show how wrong you can be.'

Hugo was cut to the quick. Later that night, when Pongwiffy was playing a rusty old mouth-organ under the moon on the mattress in the rubbish dump, he slipped out with a pair of tweezers and returned shortly afterwards with one of Dudley's whiskers draped around his neck.

''Ere,' he said. 'Zis vat you vant?'

'It certainly is!' whooped Pongwiffy. 'Oh, well done, Hugo. Does this mean you're back on the team?'

'Ja,' said Hugo. 'Today I finish ze spring-cleanink. Now I ready to make Magic!'

Pongwiffy broke into a broad grin. Hugo was back on the team, and now she had *three* of the things needed for Granny Malodour's Wishing Water. Things were looking promising. The Locke of Goldene Hayre next.

CHAPTER SEVEN

Ye Locke of Goldene Hayre

This next part of the story introduces a brand new character. Her name is Honeydimple. I don't suppose you'll like her much.

Honeydimple has big blue eyes and eyelashes which bat. She has a pert, turned-up nose and a rose-bud mouth. She wears spotlessly-clean white dresses and socks, takes three baths a day and skips around a lot, saying, 'Hello, treeth, hello, pretty birdth, good morning mithter thun,' and things like that. She also screams and kicks if she doesn't get her way.

Honeydimple's father happens to be A King. This, of course, makes Honeydimple A Princess, which is why she gets away with such unspeakable behaviour.

I forgot to mention that she also has the traditional

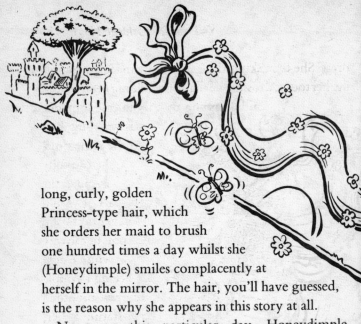

long, curly, golden
Princess-type hair, which
she orders her maid to brush
one hundred times a day whilst she
(Honeydimple) smiles complacently at
herself in the mirror. The hair, you'll have guessed,
is the reason why she appears in this story at all.

Now, on this particular day, Honeydimple, having changed into yet another clean white frock (the third that morning), decided to go for a stroll. It was boring in the Palace, because everyone was spring-cleaning. Remembering that wild strawberries were sometimes to be found in the meadow beyond the fence at the bottom of the Palace garden, off she tripped in her shiny white shoes.

(You will probably think that this is a great coincidence, Honeydimple going for a walk on the very day that Pongwiffy needed a lock of golden hair from the head of a princess. It is. So?)

Honeydimple opened the gate in the fence and stepped through, taking care not to dirty her white dress. She then skipped off down the meadow, pointing her toes and tossing her hair and holding her dress out and dimpling prettily in case someone was watching her. At the same time, she carefully avoided the cow-pats. It would never do to slip and spoil her lovely white frock. Seeing a couple of open-mouthed cows staring at her, Honeydimple outdid herself. She laughed with delight at the butterflies,

stooped to pick a bunch of wild flowers, threw them away because they made her white gloves dirty, and sang a little song about happiness. At this point, the cows rolled their eyes to heaven and returned to cropping the grass.

Deprived of her audience, Honeydimple gave a cross pout and flounced off to the wild strawberry patch.

And what should be sitting in the middle of the strawberry patch but the *cutest little Hamster imaginable*, with darling ears and pink paws and an adorable, twitchy little nose!

'A Hamthter! Oh, how thweet! Hello, cute little Hamthter. Are you lotht?'

She stretched out her hand. Quick as a flash, the cute Hamster scuttled out of reach and hid coyly beneath a dandelion leaf, peeking out shyly and blinking its beady little eyes.

'Coochy, coochy, come on, little Hamthter, don't be thy,' trilled Honeydimple, relentlessly advancing.

Hugo (for, of course, it was he) ran a short way further, almost to where the woods bordered the meadow, then stopped, looked back and simpered. Honeydimple hesitated.

'You want me to follow you? Oh, but I muthn't. Daddy thayth I muthn't go into the woodth or I'll be thure of a big thurprithe. There are *witcheth*, you know. And a dirty old rubbith tip in the middle.'

Swallowing his pride, Hugo sat on his back legs and washed his face with his paws, doing his best to look appealing.

'Oh, how thweet, how perfectly thweet! Oh,

pleathe, little Hamthter, let me pick you up. Come on, darling little Hamthter, come back to the Palathe with me . . .'

Honeydimple had nearly reached the edge of the wood now. So intent was she on capturing Hugo that she was totally unprepared for what happened next. What happened next was, a large, smelly sack came down over her and All – to cut a long story short – Went Black.

'Where am I? What happened? Have I been kidnapped?' said Honeydimple, coming round some time later. The smelly sack was no longer over her head. This was a disadvantage in one way, for it meant that she could see things. And she wasn't at all keen on what she saw.

She was bound hand and foot, tied to a table-leg in some sort of scruffy old hovel. A ragged curtain hung across the one window, and it was hard to make out much detail in the dim light. But there were some strange, clashing smells in the air – disinfectant, something like gone-off roses, and something else much more horrible.

After a few exploratory sniffs, Honeydimple tracked down the source of the particularly horrible smell. It wafted from the bundle of rags dumped in the rocking-chair opposite. Or was it a bundle of rags? No, perhaps it was a scarecrow. Hard to tell. As Honeydimple's nose wrinkled in distaste, the bundle of rags/scarecrow spoke:

'You're in my hovel,' it said. 'And what happened was, I put a sack over your head.'

Honeydimple opened her mouth and let out a shrill scream.

'Do you mind?' said the scarecrow. 'I've got a terrible headache, had it since this morning. I think it's the air-freshener. By the way, the answer to your third question is yes, you've been kidnapped.'

Honeydimple thought about this for a moment, wept a bit, then asked the obvious question. 'Why?'

'Because I happen to urgently need a lock of golden hair from a Princess's head, that's why. For a spell I'm working on.'

As evidence, the scarecrow produced a large pair of scissors and opened and closed them a couple of times with a sinister chuckle.

'Cut off a lock of my pretty hair? Thertainly not. Daddy would go mad!' said Honeydimple.

'Can't be helped. I need it,' said the scarecrow, who in fact wasn't a scarecrow at all but a squalid-looking old woman wearing a filthy cardigan beneath an even filthier cloak. Through her tears, Honeydimple made out a tall pointed hat hanging from elastic on the back of the door.

It rather seemed that she had fallen into the clutches of a Witch!

'What's more,' continued the Witch, 'I can't cut it until tonight, when the moon comes up. The recipe particularly calls for fresh hair, see. So you'll just have to be my guest for a while.'

'Out of the quethtion,' snapped Honeydimple. 'I'm not thtaying another minute in thith dirty old dump, tho there.'

If she hadn't been lying down and tied up, she would have stamped her foot. As it was, she had to make do with scowling and sticking out her bottom lip.

'You think *this* is dirty? You should have seen it

before they cleaned it,' said Pongwiffy with a nostalgic sigh. 'Now, that was what you *could* call dirt. What you're seeing is just a light coating of dust.'

'Well, it'th not what I'm uthed to at all. Untie me immediately. When Daddy getth to hear about thith he'll . . . oh, look! Thereth that little Hamthter! The one in the meadow! Tho you captured him too, you horrible old woman!'

Hugo came through the doorway, stopped, bristled and gave her a dirty look which Honeydimple completely misinterpreted.

'Oh, poor little thing! Look, he'th thivering with fear! Never mind, poor little Hamthter, we'll get away from thith nathty old Witch, don't you worry.'

'No you won't,' said Pongwiffy. 'Not until full moon.'

'I thuppothe you're keeping him ath your thlave! Fanthy forthing a poor little creature like that to do all your dirty work. Never mind, little Hamthter, when Daddy rethcueth me, thith old Witch will be thrown into the dungeon, and I'll buy you a nithe little cage all of your own. I shall call you Tiddleth and you shall be my pe —'

'Don't say it!' warned Pongwiffy. 'Don't use the "P" word. He doesn't like it. Gets right up his nose.'

Unlike Honeydimple, she recognized the warning signs. Tiddles was visibly swelling, and his eyes had gone red. His cheek pouches pulsed, his whiskers lashed and his fur stood on end. It was quite terrifying.

'Come on, Tiddleth, don't be afraid. Come over here and I'll tell you all about life in the Palathe,' went on Honeydimple blithely. 'You'll love it, really you will. I thall buy you a little wheel and teach you trickth and — jutht a minute — what are you doing?'

Hugo had suddenly snatched the scissors from Pongwiffy's lap and was advancing on her with a face like thunder. Before she knew what was happening, Honeydimple was short of a lock of golden hair.

Honeydimple gave a sharp shriek, clutched her head and burst into loud sobs.

'Oh, bother you, Hugo!' scolded Pongwiffy, leaping from her rocking-chair. 'It wasn't supposed to be cut until tonight, you idiot!'

'I not care! Zese insults I not take! She go now, or I bite 'er on ze ankle!'

'Boo hoo hoo! What did he do that for, the horrible little beatht!' bawled Honeydimple.

'Well, it's your own fault,' scolded Pongwiffy. 'He's sensitive. I warned you not to make him mad. All that talk of wheels and stuff. Like a red rag to a bull.'

'Boo hoo hoo! But I only thaid he could be my pet . . .'

That did it.

'I NOT PET! I VITCH FAMILIAR!' screeched Hugo, beside himself with rage. And, as promised, he went for the ankle.

Later that day, the Palace servants were surprised to hear a loud knocking at the front door, accompanied by a lot of distraught sobbing. Apparently, the noise had been going on for some time, but everyone was busy spring-cleaning and no one had heard it above the hoovering.

When the door was finally opened, it revealed a wild-eyed, weeping, dishevelled Honeydimple with a long, unlikely story about being lured into the woods by a mad Hamster, where she was captured by a Witch and tied up in a hovel before being set upon by the crazed Hamster again who cut her hair and bit her on the ankle and chased her through the woods and tripped her up into cow-pats and pushed her into a pig trough, all the while calling her dreadful names in some frightful foreign language.

Honeydimple's parents, King Futtout II and Queen Beryl, were sent for and gravely listened while Honeydimple told her story again. And guess what? Instead of being soundly smacked and sent to bed, she was given a bowl of strawberries and promised a pair of ice-skates and given her mother's solemn promise that Daddy would look into the matter.

Doesn't it make you sick?

CHAPTER EIGHT

Of course, all this activity wasn't going unnoticed. You can't go around snatching whiskers and falling into quicksand and getting attacked by toads and stealing feathers and kidnapping princesses without attracting a *bit* of attention.

There were thirteen Witches in Pongwiffy's Coven, and they all lived in Witchway Wood (which might look small on the map, but in some mysterious way seems to stretch to fit everyone in).

As well as the official monthly Sabbat, traditionally held on the last Friday of the month, the Witches saw quite a bit of each other on a daily basis (or nightly basis, depending on their habits). So it wasn't surprising that Pongwiffy's curious behaviour very quickly supplanted spring-cleaning as the current hot topic of conversation. As topics of conversation go, talking about Pongwiffy behind her back beat spring-cleaning hands down. The gossip spread like wildfire.

Witches Ratsnappy and Sludgegooey were sitting in Sludgegooey's kitchen having an animated discussion about a particular brand of air-freshener, when Witch Bendyshanks came rushing in.

'I say!' gasped Bendyshanks. 'Guess what? I just met Gaga and she's just seen the twins and they've just been talking to Greymatter who met Bonidle who saw Macabre who heard that Scrofula's looking for Pongwiffy *because-she-thinks-Pongwiffy-knows something-about-Barry's-stolen- feather*!'

'*No!* Really?'

'Surely *not!*'

Ratsnappy and Sludgegooey looked suitably shocked.

'Mind you, I wouldn't put it past her,' added Ratsnappy.

'True,' nodded Sludgegooey sagely. 'She's been acting very strangely since that quicksand business. Very strangely indeed.'

'I wonder what she was doing at the quicksand in the first place?' mused Ratsnappy. 'Macabre said she was very secretive about it all when Rory brought her home. She's up to something. I'm sure of it.'

'You're right,' agreed Sludgegooey. 'Come to think of it, I passed Sharkadder early this morning, running back from Malpractiss Magic with a load of bandages and a packet of plasters. I asked her if she'd

cut herself and she said something about Dudley's cheek and how she was going to pulverize Pongwiffy when she saw her.'

'And that's not all!' burst out Bendyshanks, shrill with excitement. Ratsnappy and Sludgegooey shushed her and looked over their shoulders. Bendyshanks

lowered her voice to a conspiratorial whisper. 'That's not all. My sister's boy Gary, over at the Palace, said that stuck-up Princess Honeydimple came back from the woods yesterday with a *very strange story indeed*!'

'Tell us, tell us!' urged Sludgegooey, flying to put the kettle on.

'Well, apparently, Her Royal Hoity-toityness went out into the meadow, and who should be sitting in a strawberry patch wearing his best I'm So Cute face, but . . .'

And so on.

It wasn't long before the gossip reached the ears of Grandwitch Sourmuddle, Mistress of the Coven. Or rather, it reached the small, pointy red ones of

Snoop, Sourmuddle's Demon
Familiar, who relayed it into his
mistress's ear-trumpet with relish.

'What?' said Sourmuddle irritably. Like
all the Witches (apart from Pongwiffy), she had been
spring-cleaning. Her back was killing her, egged on
by her knees. Right now, she was taking a well-
deserved breather in her favourite chair.
Her shoes were off and she
was half-way through a large
bowl of nourishing, energy-
giving Lice Crispies.

'Speak up, Snoop, I can't
hear you over me own slurping. Pongwiffy's been
what? Baking gruel?'

'Breaking rules, Sour-
muddle! Stealing whiskers. Fooling around
in quicksand. Helping herself to Barry's new tail-
feather without even a by-your-leave or may-I.
Kidnapping Princesses without filling in the proper
chit. Rumour has it she's working on a secret spell,
Sourmuddle. Without asking your permission. An
old-fashioned one, with funny ingredients.'

'Is she, by thunder? Well, we'll soon see
about that!'

Sourmuddle slammed down the bowl,

spilling milk over her clean floor. She was a stickler for the rules. Old-fashioned secret spells with funny ingredients were supposed to get special clearance from the Coven Mistress. You had to go to her with the recipe and be prepared to answer some very searching questions. After all, in the wrong hands, some of these old spells could be quite dangerous.

'I thought you'd want to know,' said Snoop smugly.

'I certainly do, Snoop. Er – know what?'

Sourmuddle's two-hundred-year-old memory let her down at times.

'About the secret spell,' Snoop reminded her.

'Yes, exactly, that's what I said,' nodded Sourmuddle, picking up the bowl and beginning to eat noisily again. 'I mean, if everyone went running around doing secret spells, badness knows what might happen. There might be all kinds of clashes.

You can't be too careful where Magic's concerned. You were quite right to tell me. What else are they saying?'

'That it's high time you gave her an official warning, Sourmuddle. And I think they're right. I think you should call a meeting at once.'

'Excellent idea! I'll leave it up to you, then, Snoop. Get a poster organized. Tonight, Emergency Meeting, Crag Hill, Midnight, Everyone Must Attend, Bring Your Own Sandwiches ... you know the sort of thing. On second thoughts, it looks like rain. Best be on the safe side and book Witchway Hall. Apart from anything else, I'm not sure my bum could take an hour's Broomstick ride tonight. Not after all that spring-cleaning.'

Just at that moment there was a knock at the door.

'Oh, goody, the postman!' exclaimed Sourmuddle, who was expecting a Bat on Elastic. For the past six weeks she had eaten Lice Crispies until they came out of her ears in order to get enough tokens. She pushed the bowl aside and scuttled to open the door. Sadly, it wasn't the postman. Instead, it was Sharkadder and Scrofula with Dudley and Barry in tow. Both Familiars sported a great deal of sticking-plaster and looked extremely sorry for themselves. Sharkadder and Scrofula were falling over themselves in their eagerness to complain about Pongwiffy.

'Sourmuddle, guess what Pongwiffy did, she stole Dudley's whisker!'

'. . . after all Barry's gone through, I think it's the absolute limit . . .'

'. . . and I'd already said she couldn't have a whisker, so what does she do, she sends that sneaky little Hamster . . .'

'. . . I mean, look at the state of him . . .'

'. . . my Dudley's terribly upset . . .'

'. . . Barry's getting legal advice, and I don't blame him . . .'

BOO HOO HOO

'. . . Pongwiffy's really gone over the top this time . . .'

'. . . and, what's more, Sourmuddle, there's a rumour that the Palace are thinking of sending a formal letter of complaint,' finished Scrofula triumphantly, 'Because of the Princess Business. Did you know about the Princess Business, Sourmuddle?'

'Certainly I know about

the Princess Business,' snapped Sourmuddle. 'I'm Grandwitch, remember? It's my business to know these things. In fact, I decided ages ago to hold an Emergency Meeting and thrash things out. Snoop is even now drafting out a poster. By the way, Snoop, I think we should send Pongwiffy an official summons and get it delivered by hand. I don't want her pretending she doesn't know about it. Now, who shall I get to take it?'

'Us!' shouted Sharkadder and Scrofula, jumping up and down and gnashing their teeth. 'Us! Send us, Sourmuddle, we'll go!'

'Certainly not,' said Sourmuddle. 'Simmer down, the pair of you. You'll go through the proper channels. You can have your say tonight at the Emergency Meeting. Send Macabre, Snoop. No, on second thoughts, perhaps not. I don't want Pongwiffy frightened off. Tell you what – send the twins.'

Snoop sent the twins.

CHAPTER NINE

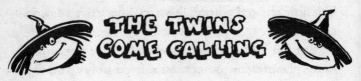

THE TWINS COME CALLING

'What d'you mean, summons?' said Pongwiffy, staring down at the official brown envelope in dismay. 'Who from? What for?'

Two identical round faces beamed at her from the doorstep.

'It's from Sourmuddle. She wants to make sure you come to the Emergency Meeting,' explained Agglebag helpfully.

'What d'you mean, Emergency Meeting?'

'It's a meeting you hold when there's a crisis,' Agglebag told her. 'Isn't that right, Bag?'

'That's exactly right, Ag. I thought you explained that beautifully,' nodded her twin Bagaggle, and they smiled at each other happily. As always, they were holding hands. On their faces were identical smiles. In their free hands, they held identical violins. Their two identical cats, IdentiKit and CopiCat, strolled past Pongwiffy's legs and sharpened their identical claws on her sofa before wandering over to

have a quiet chat with Hugo, who was neatly label-
ling little jars and putting them in Pongwiffy's Magic
cupboard.

'But I'm busy,' wailed Pongwiffy. 'I've got something planned for tonight. I can't possibly spare the
time to go to some old Emergency Meeting. What's
it about anyway?'

'Who knows?' chorused the twins, innocently rolling their eyes to heaven.

'Well, I bet it's not important. Tell Sourmuddle
I'm ill or something. Tell her I wasn't in and you
couldn't deliver the summons.'

'Ooh, we couldn't do that, could we, Ag?' said
Bagaggle, terribly shocked.

'Certainly not, Bag,' tutted Agglebag. 'That'd be
telling fibbers.'

'Sourmuddle seemed terribly keen that you
should be there, Pongwiffy. Didn't she, Ag?' added
Bagaggle.

'That's what she said, Bag,' confirmed Agglebag,
tucking her violin under her chin and playing a
hideous little discord. 'That's why she sent the summons. Just in case you didn't see the poster. Didn't
she, Bag?'

'That's right, Ag. She did. And, by the way,
Pongwiffy, you're in trouble. Sharkadder and
Scrofula are both looking for you. Aren't they, Ag?'

'They certainly are, Bag.'

'Oh, really? I can't think why,' said Pongwiffy with a light little laugh.

Up to that moment, things had been going surprisingly well. Not only was she well on her way to collecting all the main ingredients for Granny Malodour's Wishing Water, but that very morning, a large box of basic items had arrived from Sharkadder's catalogue. It contained everything Pongwiffy wanted and quite a few of the items were on special offer, so it worked out cheaper than Malpractiss Magic Inc., where the prices were so high they made your nose bleed. (Not that it made any difference, as she paid for the whole lot with the magic coin that always returns to her purse anyway, so to all intents and purposes it was free.)

Her Magic cupboard was now looking much healthier. Much to Hugo's exasperation, she had rescued the old wands and crystal balls and crumbly spell books from the rubbish dump and tenderly placed them back on their own shelves. They sat next to the rows of new, neat, winking little jars.

'Zey look out of place,' Hugo had complained.

'They do, don't they?' Pongwiffy had agreed. 'Don't worry, they'll soon dirty up nicely.'

'I not mean ze jars, I mean ze old rubbish you put

back in. How you spell Eau de Boiled Haddock?'

'Who cares? Don't interrupt me, I'm trying to think of a way of getting hold of Ye Bobble From Ye Gobline Hat. It's not going to be easy, you know. Goblins never take their hats off voluntarily because they're scared their brains'll freeze up. I know all about Goblins because I used to live next door to some.'

'I know,' said Hugo. 'You told me.'

It was at this point that there had come the rapping on the door. Agglebag and Bagaggle, come to deliver the summons and completely ruin her day.

'Aren't you going to ask us in?' inquired Bagaggle, peering hopefully past Pongwiffy into the dim recesses of the hovel. 'I think I hear a kettle boiling, don't you, Ag?'

'I do, Bag. I expect Pongwiffy will offer us a nice hot cup of bogwater.'

'No I won't,' said Pongwiffy.

'In that case, we'll stand outside and play our violins.'

'Come in,' said Pongwiffy, who knew when she was beaten.

Beaming, the twins entered. They took two identical looks at the clean, tidy hovel and their mouths fell open. Bagaggle clutched her twin's arm.

'Do my eyes deceive me, Ag, or has she been spring-cleaning?' she breathed.

'I do believe you're right, Bag. It looks lovely, Pongwiffy. What's that delightful smell?' inquired Agglebag.

'Reeka Reeka Roses,' said Pongwiffy bitterly. 'And, just for the record, I haven't lifted a finger.'

'Zat's right,' said Hugo from inside the cupboard, where he was finishing his jar-labelling. 'Me and ze Broom do it all.'

'Well, we think it's wonderful,' chorused the twins. The Broom shuffled coyly around in its corner, flushed with pride.

'I especially like the floor, don't you Ag?' said Bagaggle kindly.

'I do, Bag, I do. I've never seen it so beautifully swept. Your Broom's done a great job, Pongwiffy.'

The Broom swept a little way out of the corner and attempted a bow. Pongwiffy grabbed it and threw it outside, where it began to sweep the path importantly. The twins continued to stare around. Their beady little eyes didn't miss a thing. Bagaggle nudged Agglebag and pointed.

'By the way, over there on the table, isn't that a . . .?'

'Pigeon feather,' said Pongwiffy firmly, picking it up and throwing it hastily into the nearest cupboard. 'I collect them, you know. Now, how do you like your bogwater?'

'With biscuits,' explained Agglebag. 'Don't we, Bag?'

'That's right, Ag,' said Bagaggle, staring out of the window. 'And cake.'

'Hugo! Three cups of bogwater please. And offer the twins some of those nice home-made rock-cakes,' ordered Pongwiffy.

'Best make that five cups, Pongwiffy,' said Bagaggle.

'Huh? Why? There's you two and me. That makes three.'

'Five,' repeated Bagaggle. 'Sharkadder and Scrofula are just coming up the path. I'm sure they'd like a cup. Badness me, they do look cross. Come and see how cross they look, Pongwiffy. Pongwiffy? Where's she gone, Ag?'

'Vanished in a smelly puff of smoke, Bag,' explained Agglebag. 'Hugo's gone as well, look.'

Sure enough, there was a small, green, evil-smelling cloud hovering in the place where Pongwiffy had been standing. The door to the Magic cupboard swung open, and there was no sign of Hugo.

'Say what you like, Ag, she's fast,' said Bagaggle with an admiring little shake of the head.

'She needs to be if Sharkadder and Scrofula are on the war-path, Bag.'

'Oh, but they're not, Ag. At least, not at this very moment. I just said that to see what Pongwiffy'd do, tee hee hee.'

'Good thinking, Bag! And now we can eat all the rock-cakes.'

Chuckling, the twins helped themselves to a cake each and attempted a bite. They both looked at each other.

'Perhaps not,' they chorused.

CHAPTER TEN

THE DEMON BARBER

'Phew! That was a close one!' gasped Pongwiffy, staggering a few paces before buckling at the knees and slithering gratefully down the nearest tree.

'Ssh. Don't speak,' begged Hugo, who was lying down in a clump of grass, very pale round the pouches. 'I still vaitink for tummy to catch up.'

'The trees are whizzing round! I can't stop them! Remind me not to use that spell again,' groaned Pongwiffy, crawling off on all fours and collapsing into a nearby bush.

She had transported them into a large glade on the other side of Witchway Wood, using the first transportation spell that had come into her mind. Unfortunately, like most of Pongwiffy's spells, it was one of those old-fashioned, wonky ones which did the trick but came with nasty side-effects. It got you out of there fast, but by golly you paid for it.

They both lay quietly moaning for a while, wishing they hadn't had so much breakfast. At one point, Pongwiffy remarked that there was something familiar about that tall tree over there, the one with the rope-ladder and the red and white stripy pole, and that if only it would stay still for a moment she'd know what it was. A bit later, Hugo remarked that he would sooner have taken his chances with Sharkadder and Scrofula. On the whole, Pongwiffy was inclined to agree with him.

It was fate, of course. One chance in a million. But things like fate and coincidence and one-in-a-million chances are always cropping up in Witchway Wood. There they were, Pongwiffy and Hugo, lying down quietly, conveniently hidden by grass and bushes, when who should come along the path but . . .

THE GOBLINS! Yes, here they come, all seven of them, stomping along in single file. Plugugly, Stinkwart, Eyesore, Slopbucket, Sproggit, Hog and Lardo. Those are their names. They live in a damp cave on a particularly horrible mountain which borders the south-west edge of Witchway Wood. Right now, they are off on one of their doomed-to-failure hunting trips. You can tell this because their faces are smeared with soot, they are carrying the traditional Goblin Hunting-bags (the ones with the traditional holes cut in the bottom) and they are singing a loud hunting song:

'*Oh, a-hunting we will go,*' sang the Goblins, horribly out of tune,

'A-hunting we will go,
We'll bump the trees
And hurt our knees
And then we'll stub our toe.'

'Well, well, well,'
hissed Pongwiffy, suddenly alert
and cured of all queasiness. 'What have
we here?'

'Goblins!' gloated Hugo, also perking up considerably. 'Ve in luck, Mistress. Vat ve do? Jump out at
zem and grab ze bobbles off zere 'ats?'

'No. I don't want to draw any more attention to
myself. We've got to be subtle. Stay hidden. I want
to watch. I wonder why they're out hunting today?
It's not Tuesday, is it?'

(Tuesday is the Goblin's traditional hunting night. They rarely come down into Witchway Wood at any other time, because Witches and Goblins don't like each other. The Witches think the Goblins are stupid and the Goblins think the Witches are spiteful. They both have a point.)

The Goblins rounded the corner, and further conversation was impossible. Apart from anything else, you couldn't hear yourself speak above the dreadful singing!

'*A-hunting we will go,*' warbled the Goblins.

> *'A-hunting we will go,*
> *We'll trip on logs*
> *And drown in bogs*
> *And then . . .'*

'Halt!' shouted the Goblin at the front, doing it. There was a squeezed concertina effect as the Goblins piled up on each other, shouting alarmed cries of, 'What dat?' and, 'What happenin' up front there, Plugugly?' and, 'Is we attacked?'

'I gettin' tired o' dis song,' explained Plugugly, who was the Goblin at the front. He usually got stuck at the front, not because of his powers of leadership but because he was the biggest and therefore best equipped to carve a path when the going got rough. Like a snow-plough, but more stupid.

'What you mean, tired of it?' objected Eyesore. 'We've only sung it eighty-free times. 'Ow can you be tired of it?'

'Well, I am,' insisted Plugugly stubbornly. 'It depressin' me. All dis talk o' hurtin' knees and fallin' in bogs an' dat. I fink we should sing anudder one. Fer a change.'

'We don't know anuvver huntin' song,' pointed out Hog.

'Ah, but we ain't *really* goin' huntin', so it don't 'ave

ter be a huntin' song, do it?' remarked Slopbucket, who was immediately rounded on and soundly criticized.

'Ssh! Idiot!'

'We said we wasn't goin' ter say nuffin, remember?'

''E's blown the gaff!'

'Talk about mouf, you could lose a battleship in 'is mouf!'

'Sorry,' said Slopbucket, going red, aware of his indiscretion the minute he had said it. 'Slipped out. Sorry.'

'We could sing "'Ere We Go",' suggested young Sproggit, hopping from boot to boot in his eagerness. 'One o' my favourites, that.'

''Ows it go again?' asked Hog. 'I've forgotten the words.'

''Ere we go, 'ere we go, 'ere we go,' supplied Sproggit. ''Ere we go, 'ere we go, 'ere we go-oh, 'ere we go, 'ere we go, 'ere we go, 'ere we go-oh, 'ere we go . . .'

'Oh yeah,' said Hog. 'I remember now.'

'Acherly, there ain't no point in singin' anyfin',' remarked Stinkwart. 'Cos we've arrived. We're 'ere. 'Oo's gonna ring the bell?'

This was the cue for all the Goblins to huddle together in terror and try to push each other to the front. Apparently, no one wanted to ring the bell.

'Vat zey do?' whispered Hugo from behind his grass. 'Vy zey frightened?'

'I don't know,' muttered Pongwiffy. 'But I tell you one thing. I've suddenly recognized that tree over there! The tall one with the rope-ladder and the stripy pole sticking out, see? Come to think of it, that pole never used to be there. But it's definitely the same tree. There's a tree-house right up the top of that tree, and I happen to know who lives there.'

'Oh. Who?'

'A nasty little Tree Demon, that's who. Did I ever tell you about the awful experience I had when I was house-hunting? It was all Sharkadder's fault. This is before your time, of course . . .'

'Ssh,' said Hugo. 'Look.'

By some mysterious process known as Pushing, the Goblins had unanimously elected Plugugly as official bell-ringer. Unwillingly, with much hesita-

tion and backward glancing, he approached the tall tree with the rope-ladder, the one that Pongwiffy recognized despite the addition of the mysterious striped pole, and gave the bell-rope that hung there a reluctant little tug. At once, an almighty clanging sounded high up in the branches. Plugugly staggered back a step, dropped the bell-rope as if scalded and ran back to the doubtful safety of the group.

'Coming, sir, coming, sir, just one minute if you *please*!' came the bad-tempered screech from on

high. The foot of the rope-ladder shook, there was a flash of green, and suddenly a small Tree Demon was standing at the foot of the tree. He wore a white coat with a large breast pocket which contained an assortment of vicious looking knives, razors, scissors and combs. His pinched green face wore an expression of extreme irritation.

'Yes?' he shrieked. 'What can I do for you, gentlemen?'

'I don't believe it!' gasped Pongwiffy. 'Now I've seen everything! The knife-happy little stinker's gone and set himself up as a Demon Barber!'

CHAPTER ELEVEN

YE BOBBLE OFF YE HAT OF A GOBLINE

'And how would sir like it?' threatened the Tree Demon, tapping his foot, rolling his eyes and whetting his razor impatiently.

Plugugly cleared his throat unhappily and didn't say a thing. He had been forced at comb-point to sit on a stump in the middle of the glade. He had been heavily draped in a towel. The traditional saucepan he always wore on his head had been forcibly removed and placed out of reach on a nearby branch. He felt terribly insecure without it.

'Well?' prompted the Tree Demon, who didn't suffer fools gladly.

Plugugly licked his lips and tried to think whilst the Tree Demon climbed up behind him on a handy log and clashed a huge pair of scissors experimentally in the air. The rest of the Goblins stood around and stared in open-mouthed horror.

(Goblins have a terrible fear of having their hair

cut. For them, having their hair cut is sissy stuff which falls into the same category as washing. They hate it so much, they only do it once a year. When the time of The Haircut rolls round again, they get into a terrible state. They are so convinced that everyone will laugh at them that they try to keep the whole venture undercover. That's why they were pretending to be going hunting, so no one would know where they were really going.)

'Come along, come along, come along, come along sir, *if you please*!' spat the Tree Demon. As a hairdresser, his sinkside manner left a lot to be desired. 'There's other gentlemen waiting, you know.'

'I want it long,' Plugugly suddenly burst out. 'Long an' greasy!'

'I see,' nodded the Tree Demon, stroking his chin professionally. 'Long and greasy. Anything else, sir?'

'Sideburns,' instructed Plugugly, suddenly hopeful. Adding, 'An' one o' dem wotsits – quiffs.'

'Right away, sir,' said the Tree Demon. 'See the match by any chance last night?'

'Eh?' said Plugugly.

'Never mind, never mind. It's just something we Demon Barbers always say. Keep still.'

The scissors flashed, and in seconds Plugugly was

the horrified owner of the
shortest back and sides it is
possible to have without being
pronounced clinically bald. The general effect was
of huge jug-handles stuck on either side of a crimson
pimple. The watching Goblins all gasped, pointed,
then disloyally fell about laughing.

Behind their bush, Pongwiffy and Hugo did the
same.

'There we are, sir,' said the Tree Demon, simultaneously flashing a mirror around, snatching the
towel away and picking Plugugly's pocket. 'Very
nice, very smart, that. Don't forget your saucepan,
sir. Pay on your way out. Next!'

The Goblins immediately sobered up. Nobody
wanted to be next.

'You,' hissed the Tree Demon, pointing at Lardo,
who had been laughing louder than anyone.

'Me?' gulped Lardo, quaking. (He probably had
an even bigger morbid fear of being
parted from his hat than the rest of
the Goblins. It was his comforter.
He needed it. He sucked the
bobble when he went to sleep.
He had lost it once, and all sorts
of bad things had happened.)
'Yes, you! The short, fat, stupid

one with the bobble hat. Take your hat off, place it on the branch and get over here. I haven't got all day.'

'This is it,' mouthed Pongwiffy to Hugo. 'Now's our chance!'

Poor Lardo. Slowly he shuffled forward, removed his hat with trembling hands and hung it carefully on the branch next to Plugugly's saucepan, as instructed. He then reluctantly approached the dreaded stump where the scissor-happy Tree Demon was holding out the towel and flapping it like a toreador.

'What's it to be, sir?' asked the Tree Demon, tucking Lardo up firmly and menacing him with a large pot of shaving-cream. 'The Usual?'

Lardo whispered something.

'Speak up, sir, speak up if you *please*!' said the Tree Demon.

'Curls,' said Lardo, and blushed.

'Certainly, certainly. Would that be *golden* curls?'

Lardo confirmed that, yes, golden curls would be most acceptable.

'Golden Curls coming right up, sir. Shocking weather we been having,' observed the Tree Demon, and went to work. In no time at all, Lardo emerged with the second short back and sides of the day. This time, it was Plugugly's turn to laugh until he was sick.

'There we are, sir, lovely cut, that!' insisted the Tree Demon, trying to force Lardo to look at himself in the mirror.

Lardo gave a little sob, threw off the towel and ran the gauntlet past the hysterical Goblins to where his beloved hat hung on the tree. He snatched it up and was about to ram it on, when he suddenly noticed something.

'All right, who's got it?' he asked plaintively. 'Enough's enough. You've gone too far this time. Who's the joker what's taken me bobble? Eh? Eh?'

Needless to say, nobody owned up.

Back at Number One, Dump Edge, Pongwiffy and Hugo were celebrating. Pongwiffy was dancing on the table doing a wild Spanish dance, Lardo's bobble clutched between her teeth like a wilting rose.

'We got it! We got the bobble!' she crowed. 'I just can't believe our luck, Hugo. It's almost as though it's meant to be. Put the kettle on, I fancy a huge mug of bogwater with three sugars to celebrate. No sign of Ag and Bag. Or Sharky and

Scrofula, for that matter. I wonder where they've all got to?'

'Who knows?' said Hugo. 'It look like ze twins leave in hurry. Zey not drink ze bogwater. Only two bites out of rock-cakes.'

(In fact, the twins were currently sitting in a dentist's waiting-room. Bagaggle was waiting to have a piece of Pongwiffy's rock-cake chiselled from between her teeth, and Agglebag was holding her hand and reading out soothing horoscopes from old back-issues of Witch's Realm.)

'They've left the summons, though,' said Pongwiffy, pointing at the ominous brown envelope with a little sigh. There was always something that had to spoil things.

'Aren't you going to open it?' asked Hugo curiously.

Pongwiffy carefully placed the precious bobble in her Magic cupboard, alongside Dudley's whisker, the quicksand, Barry's feather and Honeydimple's hair. She then picked up the brown envelope and opened it. Inside was a piece of paper.

It said:

I SUMMON YOU to APPEAR at Tonight's MEETING & THAT'S AN ORDER

SOURMUDDLE

'Huh,' said Pongwiffy. 'What a cheek. Sourmuddle's really throwing her weight around these
days. You know what I'm going to do about *that*,
don't you?'

'Vat?' asked Hugo, eyes round.

'Go to the meeting,' said Pongwiffy lamely.

CHAPTER TWELVE

Witchway Hall is the focal point of community life in Witchway Wood. It is used for parties, Ping-Pong and protest meetings. It is also used for fund-raising events and theatrical performances. In a typical week, there might be a rabble-rousing meeting of the Hamsters Are Angry Movement (HAM) chaired by Hugo, the finals of the Lady Ghoul's Darts Championships, a Witchway Rhythm Boys' practice session, Troll country dancing (interesting), a Zombie jumble sale, a Banshee concert, a rehearsal of the Skeleton Amateur Dramatics Society (SAD), a Friends Of The Goblins Reunion Dinner (always poorly attended) and the ever-popular Beginner's Class in Demon Basket Weaving run by Snoop on wet Sunday afternoons.

In view of its popularity, the Witches were lucky to get Witchway Hall at such short notice. Normally, at midnight on a Tuesday, the Gnome

Debating Society would have been in full swing. Well, actually, it wasn't so much *luck*. It was more that Snoop had a few words in the chief Gnome Debater's ear. Nothing unpleasant, you understand, just a few quiet words about Witches and Tuesday Nights and the Importance Of Emergency Meetings and the Inconvenience Of Being Turned Into A Frog and so on.

For once, the chief Gnome Debater didn't argue.

So. There they were in Witchway Hall. It was midnight, it looked like rain, just as Sourmuddle had predicted and the Emergency Meeting was due to start.

Thirteen chairs had been set around the long trestle-table. Eleven were already occupied by Witches' bums. Well, to be strictly correct, only nine had actual bums on. Witch Gaga was standing on her head on the tenth, and Witch Macabre wasn't sitting down yet. But her bagpipes were, which was almost as bad. Various Witch Familiars were skulking, slithering and generally milling around, according to their disposition.

Sourmuddle hadn't yet arrived.

There was also no sign of Pongwiffy.

Sharkadder and Scrofula had come early and grabbed the seats on either side of Sourmuddle's chair. It was plain that they were terribly put out.

They both sat in stony silence with their arms folded and their noses in the air, refusing to join in the general chit-chat, and Barry and Dudley did likewise. All about them buzzed tantalizing talk of spells and spring-cleaning and recipes and who was hot favourite to win the Spell of the Year Competition and the trouble with Brooms today and so on, but nothing could tempt them to relax. As the injured parties, they were determined to milk the Emergency Meeting for all it was worth.

To be sure, Scrofula and Barry didn't look well at all. Scrofula's hair was greasier than ever, and her shoulders looked like the wastes of Greenland. Barry hunched mournfully on the back of her chair and tried to ignore the draught around his rear end. Every so often he shook his head slowly, sighed, said, 'Why me?' in a small, dry voice, then gave a pathetic little cough. On top of everything, he had another cold coming on.

In contrast, Sharkadder was rather enjoying all the drama. She had gone to a great deal of trouble to make herself up as a tragic victim. She was all in black, and had painted dark panda shadows beneath her eyes. Every so often she dabbed at them dramatically with a black lace hanky. Deadeye Dudley crouched vengefully at her feet, muttering dark curses and glaring balefully around, daring anyone to say one word, just one word, that's all, about his bad cheek.

Agglebag and Bagaggle were there, telling a dental horror story to anyone who cared to listen. That didn't include Greymatter, who was sitting next to them, busily writing a poem in an old exercise book. Speks, her Owl Familiar, peered thoughtfully over her shoulder and made creative suggestions every so often.

'. . . and we think Pongwiffy left the rock-cakes to tempt us on purpose, so that Bag would break her tooth!' finished up Agglebag. 'What do you think, Greymatter?'

'I beg your pardon?' said Greymatter. 'What did you say, Agglebag? I'm trying to write a poem here, if you don't mind.'

Further down the table, Sludgegooey, Ratsnappy and Bendyshanks were playing cards. Bonidle, as always, was collapsed face down on the table, fast asleep. Over by the door, Witch Macabre was having a loud argument with the caretaker, a sullen Troll by the name of Clifford. The row appeared to be about the state of the tea-urn, although they were both bellowing so loudly no one could be sure.

Several curious hangers-on skulked in the shadowy background. A couple of Skeletons lurked in the darkness of the back stalls. A few Ghouls and the

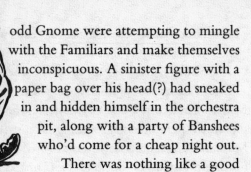

odd Gnome were attempting to mingle with the Familiars and make themselves inconspicuous. A sinister figure with a paper bag over his head(?) had sneaked in and hidden himself in the orchestra pit, along with a party of Banshees who'd come for a cheap night out.

There was nothing like a good Emergency Meeting to bring them all out of the woodwork.

'All right, settle down, settle down!' Sourmuddle came bustling in with a thermos, a bag of boiled sweets, her reading glasses and the rule book. Snoop walked behind carrying a plastic bin-liner full of essentials.

'No, no, don't bother to stand,' ordered Sourmuddle, as a few Witches made a half-hearted attempt to rise. 'This isn't a proper Coven meeting, we can dispense with the formalities, it says so in the rule book. Just sit up straight and shut up. All non-Witches out!'

Immediate consternation in the shadows. Sourmuddle held firm.

'Yes, I'm talking to you Ghouls over there. And you lot hiding in the orchestra pit, don't think I can't see you. This is a private meeting. Witches and Witch Familiars only.'

The Banshees set up an indignant caterwauling.

'It doesn't say so on the poster,' protested the Odd Gnome.

'I don't care about the poster,' said Sourmuddle firmly. 'I make the rules around here, and this is a private Witch meeting. Out. Make sure they go, Macabre. That includes you, Clifford. By the way, I hope you've cleaned out that tea-urn?'

Grumbling, the banished ones were chased from the hall by Witch Macabre, to a chorus of catcalls, raspberries and mocking laughter.

'Right,' said Sourmuddle as soon as the door had banged on them. 'Are we all here? Then sit down, Macabre, and let's get cracking.'

'I don't believe we *are* all here actually, Sourmuddle,' remarked Sharkadder with asperity, pointing to the one remaining empty chair. 'Correct me if I'm wrong, but I believe I'm right in saying that Pongwiffy's not here. Which is exactly what Scrofula and I expected, of course, and why we're disappointed you didn't give us permission to go round and pulverize her this afternoon, like we wanted to. Right, Scrofula?'

'Right, Sharkadder.'

'Sit down, Sharkadder. We'll conduct this meeting in a proper manner,' ordered Sourmuddle sharply. 'Pongwiffy's got a right to tell us her side of the story. We've only got your word for it that she stole Dudley's whisker to put in some secret spell or other.'

'But she's not coming, Sourmuddle! Don't you see?' shrieked Sharkadder. 'Even though you made a special point of telling her, she's *not coming*! She's afraid to face the music.'

'What music?' said a voice from the wings. 'Sorry I'm late, Sourmuddle. Couldn't get my Broomstick started. It's the damp. Poor thing's got a terrible cough. Keep meaning to get it seen to, but you know how it is. 'Evening, girls. Have I missed much?'

Cheerfully, Pongwiffy approached the table and plonked herself down in the one empty chair. Hugo rode as always on   the brim of her hat. He

winked cheekily down at Dudley, who flicked his tail and looked the other way. Barry gave him a long, hurt, sorrowful look, then pointedly turned his back.

'So,' said Pongwiffy. 'What's all this about facing music? I'll face anything but Ag and Bag playing violins. I had enough of that earlier. Did you enjoy the rock-cakes, you two? Sorry I had to leave a bit smartish, I just remembered something I had to do.'

'That's enough of the chit-chat, Pongwiffy,' said Sourmuddle severely. 'I'm just about to start this meeting, if you don't mind.'

'Certainly, Sourmuddle, certainly. I'm sure I don't want to hold things up longer than necessary. I'm as keen to get away early as the next Witch. By the way, what's it all about? What's so important that it

can't wait till next Sabbat? Some of us have got things to do.'

'So I've heard,' said Sourmuddle tartly. 'In fact, Pongwiffy, rumour has it that you've been doing rather too much lately. That's why we're holding this Emergency Meeting. I've been getting complaints. About you. In fact, I've got a whole list of charges against you.'

'No!' cried Pongwiffy. 'Me? Surely not!'

'Don't put on an act, Pong. You know you're collecting the ingredients for a secret spell!' shrieked Sharkadder, pointing an accusatory talon. 'We're not that stupid, are we, Scrofula?'

'We certainly are not,' agreed Scrofula, shaking her head vigorously and causing another avalanche to cascade on to her shoulders.

'You stole my Dudley's whisker, you did, Pongwiffy, and I'm going to get you for it!' screeched Sharkadder. Pongwiffy tried her best to look innocent. No one was taken in.

'Sit down, Sharkadder, before Macabre throws you out!' commanded Sourmuddle, putting on her reading glasses and holding an old envelope with notes on at arm's length. 'Do you deny, Pongwiffy, that in the past few days you've stolen or arranged to have stolen a whisker belonging to one Deadeye Dudley, misappropriated a feather belonging to one

Barry Vulture, and kidnapped that awful Princess Honeydimple against her will and hacked her hair off?'

'I categorically deny everything,' said Pongwiffy, and immediately came out in green spots. This always happened when she told fibs. It was a terrible nuisance.

'You see? You see? Look at her fib rash!' squawked Sharkadder. 'She *is* working on a secret spell, Sourmuddle, I know it! She's taking advantage of everyone being so busy doing spring-cleaning that we won't notice!'

'Aye!' chipped in Macabre. 'Why else would she want quicksand? I mean, nobody uses quicksand any more, do they? Quicksand's old-fashioned. Only very old spells call for quicksand.'

That was the signal for everyone else to join in.

'All those peculiar things she wanted in Mal-practiss Magic, I mean it stands to reason . . .'

'Skulking around all hours of the day and night, avoiding everybody . . .'

'And what about my Barry's feather? Don't forget that . . .'

'Yes, and do you know, I've seen her . . .'

'Obviously hiding something . . .'

'Attacking us with rock-cakes and vanishing in a puff of smoke . . .'

Pongwiffy listened to it all with growing alarm. It seemed that everyone had a complaint against her. Nobody was on her side. Even Greymatter's poem was about her and was distinctly unflattering. It went like this:

Uplift thee, muse! And tell how old Pongwiffy
(A witch who has a smell distinctly iffy)
Has taken things that were not hers to take;
a feather, hair, a whisker and some cake.

'I didn't take any cake!' protested Pongwiffy, but nobody heard her except Greymatter, who mumbled something about poetic licence. It seemed that everybody was trying to outdo everyone else in telling stories about her which would get her into trouble. The general feeling was definitely anti-Pong. This could have been out of sympathy for the injured parties, but was far more likely to have been because Witches are mean old hags who like picking on people.

'Order! Order! That's enough,' commanded Sour-muddle. 'Deny it all you like, Pongwiffy, but in my opinion there's an airtight case against you. It's clear as crystal balls that you're working on a secret spell.'

'All right,' cried Pongwiffy. 'All right, so I am! I admit it! But so what? We're Witches, aren't we? We're supposed to be working on spells, remember? Not polishing the silver and washing-up! Spring-cleaning's for sissies!'

There was a lot of angry muttering. Some of the loudest came from the brim of her hat. Even Hugo wasn't with her on this one.

'Ah,' said Sourmuddle. '*Spells*, yes. But *secret* spells? Not without clearing it with me first.'

'But . . .'

'It's in the rule book. Paragraph nine, item four-teen: No Pinching Items From Fellow Witches Or Their Familiars To Use In Spells Unless Given Express Permission By Grandwitch. And I certainly don't recall giving you permission. What is it, anyway? What does it do, this spell of yours? Where did you get it from?'

'I'm sorry, I'm afraid I'm not at liberty to tell you that,' said Pongwiffy.

'Oh really? Well, in that case, I'm going to ban you. Hand over your Magic Licence, Pongwiffy.'

'But . . .'

'No more buts. Hand it over. That's an order.'

There was quite a bit of unsympathetic tittering as Pongwiffy reached into her rags and drew out an old, crumpled, yellowing piece of paper. With a sulky sniff she handed it to Sourmuddle, who examined it at arm's length through her reading glasses.

'Hmm. As I thought. Two endorsements already. Right, I'm adding a third. That means you're banned from making magic of any kind, secret or otherwise, for *one whole week*!'

'But, Sourmuddle . . .' protested Pongwiffy.

'Not only that,' continued Sourmuddle sternly, 'You will also go and say you are humbly sorry to everyone you've offended. You will write a grovelling note to King Futtout apologizing for kidnapping that ghastly daughter of his. Plus you will come and clean my boots every morning for the next six weeks. That'll teach you to not clear things with me first. Right, that's settled. Meeting over. Whoopee! Sandwich time! Who wants to see my Bat on Elastic?'

Everyone did except Pongwiffy.

CHAPTER THIRTEEN

RONALD

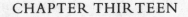

Sharkadder's nephew Ronald was feeling delighted with himself. Feeling delighted with himself was not a new sensation. Ronald was the sort of person who usually felt delighted with himself. However, right now he felt *particularly* delighted, and the reason for this was that he had just been hired by the Palace! His first proper job.

Imagine! A Royal Wizard already, and he'd only just qualified. Ten bags of gold a year, two weeks' paid holiday, expense account, turret of his own, as much as he could eat and drink and the possibility of the Princess's hand in marriage! And all he had to do in return was to do something about the Witches in Witchway Wood. Apparently, the old girls had been getting above themselves recently, and the King (Futtout II) was anxious that they should be made to tow the line.

Do something about the Witches? Nothing to it! Why, his own aunt was one! He'd simply have a word with Aunt Sharky, get her to speak severely to some of her more boisterous cronies and Bob's your uncle – or , rather, Sharky's your aunt, ha ha – he'd got it made! What could be easier?

The interview with King Futtout had gone without a hitch. It had been more a case of Ronald interviewing the King than the King interviewing Ronald.

'Are you . . . erm . . . sure you've got enough experience, Mister . . . erm . . .?' King Futtout had quavered, fixing him with anxious, wet, spaniel eyes. Futtout was small and thin and droopy and ineffectual. He didn't really speak, he just apologized. He was the sort of person who says, 'Awfully sorry' to you when you stand on his foot.

'Absolutely!' Ronald had replied grandly. He had

just caught sight of his reflection in the throne-room mirror. He knew he looked good. He was wearing the eye-catching, traditional red and purple tall pointy Hat of Knowledge and the matching ceremonial Robe of Mystery. His Mystic Staff was in his hand, and thrown casually over his shoulders was his Cloak of Darkness, the one with the star-spangled dark-blue lining which he'd paid an arm and a leg for.

His face had recently been trying very hard to grow a beard, and he was almost sure he could see the beginnings of a wisp on his chin. Best of all, much to his relief, his spots had responded well to the evil-smelling spot cream Aunt Sharkadder had sent him in the post.

Yes. He looked good all right.

Looking so good made him even more confident than usual (which was very confident indeed).

'No probs, honestly. Do something about the Witches, you say? Nothing to it. I'm an expert with Witches. Hey, listen, when we Wizards snap our fingers, those Witches jump, right? I'm your man. Bank on it. Absolutely.'

'It's just . . . erm . . . experience . . . bit young, perhaps . . . you know . . .? . . . confess I haven't actually heard of Mighty Ronald the Magnificent . . . erm?' worried King Futtout.

'I've just qualified,' explained Ronald. 'I got honours. Don't worry, I'm up to the job. I'm a member of the Wizards' Club, they all know me up there. You want to see my certificate?'

'Oh no, no, that won't be necessary . . . erm . . . I'll just have to clear things with Beryl, my . . . erm . . . wife,' King Futtout apologized. 'The Queen, that is. You know how it is? I've never appointed a Wizard before . . . not sure what to look for . . . erm . . . ha ha . . . erm . . .?'

'Sure, sure. Absolutely. Fine by me. Go right ahead. Wheel her in.'

'And my daughter?' begged King Futtout, ringing his hands. 'You don't mind if I just . . . erm . . . have a quick word . . . erm . . . with Honeydimple? She expects to be . . . erm. Consulted. Erm . . . mind of her own, you know how it is with these girls nowadays, ha ha . . . erm . . .?'

'Be my guest,' said Ronald graciously. 'I wouldn't mind a quick look at her anyway. If I'm having her hand in marriage.'

King Futtout looked unhappy, opened his mouth to speak, then closed it again and gently rang a little bell which sat on his desk. After a painfully long pause, a flunkey sauntered in with his hands in his pockets. The King apologized for bothering him and asked if he could possibly erm Queen Beryl and, if it wasn't too much trouble erm Princess Honeydimple and ask them to erm.

The servant wandered away, and Ronald and the King stared at each other and tried to think of something to break the embarrassing silence.

'So. These witches,' Ronald said. 'Been giving you a spot of trouble, have they?'

'They most certainly have,' confessed King Futtout with a little shiver. 'Just my luck the Palace backs on to Witchway Wood. That's where they all live, you know. I wish they didn't. I'm terrified of them. As a matter of fact, I'm getting quite desperate. Hiring a Wizard was all I could think of. This latest nasty business with Honeydimple . . . most upsetting . . .'

'Quite, quite, absolutely, tut tut,' sympathized Ronald. He refrained from mentioning that his aunt was a Witch. Having a Witch in the family wasn't something you boasted about. Especially if you were a Wizard. Wizards always looked down on Witches. It was traditional.

'. . . you see, stealing from the herb garden I can take,' King Futtout was saying. 'I don't even make a fuss when they buzz the turrets with their Broomsticks at night. I put up with the sound of their cackling and the awful smells drifting over from their brews – and you should try being here when the wind's in the East! And as for that rubbish dump . . .'

Ronald gave a solemn
nod. He too had smelt
Pongwiffy's tip.

'I've said nothing about
what their bats have done
to the coach paintwork and what their cats have
done to the lawn,' continued King Futtout, on the
verge of tears. 'I even turn a blind eye when that
Haggis creature with the orange fringe comes and
practises backstroke in the royal swimming-pool.
But kidnapping the Princess and setting a Hamster
on her is quite another matter, don't you think?'

'Oh, yes,' agreed Ronald. 'Absolutely. Definitely
out of order. Er – did you say Hamster?'

'Yes. Small, golden Hamster with a stupid accent.
Cut her hair off and bit her ankles. A shocking bully
she said it was.'

There was a long pause.

'Oh, all right, I know it sounds unlikely,' said
King Futtout. 'Honeydimple exaggerating again I
suppose. I wouldn't make a fuss myself, of course,
but the wife . . . Queen Beryl, that is . . . Look, I'd
be grateful if you didn't mention the . . . erm . . .
the, you know, hand in marriage business? To
Honeydimple? Not at this stage you . . . erm . . . you
understand?'

'Oh, quite,' said Ronald. 'Right. Absolutely.'

'They're making me write an official letter of complaint,' confessed King Futtout worriedly. 'Beryl and Honeydimple, that is. They want me to send it to the erm. Coven leader.'

'Grandwitch,' Ronald told him. 'She's called the Grandwitch.'

'Oh . . . erm? Frankly . . . erm . . . I'm a bit nervous.'

'May I see?' asked Ronald. 'Glance over it? Professional eye, so to speak?'

'Oh, erm, erm, of course!' cried King Futtout, scrabbling in his desk and coming up with an old envelope which he thrust gratefully into Ronald's hand.

'Is it too . . . erm . . . strong, do you think?' he asked, anxiously searching Ronald's face as he read it. 'I mean, they are Witches. I don't want to, you know. Erm. Upset them.'

'Not strong enough,' said Ronald, shaking his head. 'Not strong enough by half. You need to be firm with Witches. Where you say you're "a bit annoyed", I mean, it hardly sounds as though you're putting your foot down, does it?'

'Erm,' said King Futtout woefully. 'Erm . . . no, I suppose it doesn't.'

'Don't you worry,' Ronald reassured him. 'Leave it all to me. I can deal with Witches all right.'

'Nothing would make me happier than leaving it all to you,' admitted King Futtout longingly. 'I just hope Beryl and Honeydimple agree. I wonder where they can be?'

It transpired that Queen Beryl was visiting her mother, and had been there for the past week. Nobody had bothered to inform the King. So Ronald was spared the experience of being interviewed by her. (Just as well. Queen Beryl was a very different kettle of fish.)

Honeydimple turned up an embarrassing two hours later. 'Hello ... erm ... darling, sorry to bother you,' said King Futtout when she flounced into the room. 'Come and give Daddy a kiss. This is the Mighty Ronald the Erm.'

'Who?' snarled Honeydimple. She was wearing a grubby dressing-gown, a large straw hat (to disguise the fact that she had a huge hank of hair missing) and a petulant expression. She didn't even bother to bat her eyelashes. It was clear that she was far from over her distressing experience.

'Magnificent,' Ronald told her firmly. 'Ronald the Magnificent.'

She wasn't what he expected at all. For a start, she was years too young for him. Just a kid. And even when she grew up, he didn't think he could take that hat. Or that pout.

'Ronald's going to be our new Wizard,' explained King Futtout anxiously. 'Daddy's thinking of hiring him. I've told him all about your . . . erm . . . you know . . . Dreadful Experience. He says he can handle Witches. With him at the . . . erm . . . helm, we should have no more trouble. Right, Ronald?'

'Absolutely no probs,' agreed Ronald airily.

'There you are, you see, sweetheart. So. What d'you . . . erm . . . think of him?'

'Yeuk,' said Honey-dimple, wrinkling her nose. 'He'th got thpotth. Yeuk.'

It was at that point that Ronald decided he wasn't the marrying kind.

CHAPTER FOURTEEN
TEA AT SHARKY'S

'It's awfully nice of you to invite me and Hugo to tea, Sharky,' said Pongwiffy, surreptitiously poking her finger into the trifle. Sharkadder was too busy running to and fro between the larder, the mirror and the overflowing table to notice. 'After everything we've done. The whisker and that. We're most grateful. Aren't we, Hugo?'

'Hmm? Oh, ja,' agreed Hugo vaguely, his eyes on a bowl of bright-green frog jelly sprinkled with ants'-eggs in the form of an artistic R (for Ronald).

'Oh, that's all right, Pong,' said Sharkadder, trying to find room for a fungus sponge. 'You've suffered enough. I forgive you. Dudley hasn't, but I'm sure he'll come round.'

They all glanced at Dudley's basket. Right now, it was empty of Dudley, who had stormed out in disgust the minute he had heard that Pongwiffy and Hugo had been invited to Sunday tea after all. In fact, there had been quite a row about it. It had gone something like this:

DUDLEY: (*shocked disbelief*) *Tea*? After pinchin' my whisker, you've gone and invited 'em ter *tea*?

SHARKADDER: (*uncomfortably*) Yes, yes, don't go on about it.

DUDLEY: (*still incredulous*) *Today*? Tea *today*? With *Ronald* coming?

SHARKADDER: (*irritably*) Well, what was I supposed to do? I mean, she said she was sorry, you saw her, and she got down on all fours and blubbed on my knees! I had to think of my stockings. Besides, she is my best friend. I think we should show a little forgiveness to our best friends. After making them suffer terribly first, of course. That goes without saying.

DUDLEY: Forgiveness? But us be in the Witch business! Whatever 'appened to Vengeance?

SHARKADDER: (*piously*) We've had quite enough Vengeance, Dudley. Actually, I don't mind admitting it, I feel quite sorry for her. Just think. Banned, Dudley. Another endorsement on her licence and banned from making Magic for a *whole week*! I've invited her to tea to cheer her up and, quite frankly, I don't know what you're making such a fuss about. It's not as if it was your only whisker. I mean, you've got plenty more.

DUDLEY: (*leaving in outrage*) That does it. I'm off.

The row had happened hours ago, and Sharkadder hadn't seen him since. It was now nearly tea-time. Pongwiffy had arrived early as usual (in the middle of lunch, actually) and was sitting at the table snaffling food as Sharkadder bustled to and fro with trifles and tarts and dainty little sandwiches with the crusts cut off and jugs of yellow custard and a big cake with WELCOME RONALD picked out in green icing.

'What time is Ronald coming?' Pongwiffy asked innocently, scooping a jam tart into her mouth.

'Any time now.'

'Oh good,' said Pongwiffy. 'And how are his spots these days?'

Sharkadder stopped with a plateful of bat biscuits and gave her a warning look.

'That's quite enough of that,' she scolded. 'You be polite to Ronald, do you hear? He's a real Wizard now, he's passed his exams. He's going places, and I won't have him mocked.'

Just at that moment, there came three loud, important-sounding knocks at the door. They weren't the sort of knocks to ignore. They were knocks of substance. Stern, Open-Up-I-Haven't-Got-All-Day sort of knocks. The knocks of a Wizard who had passed his exams and expected to go places.

'That'll be him now!' cried Sharkadder, spinning round in a tizzy. 'Oh dear! He's early! Is my hair all right? Is my nose shiny? Go and answer the door, Pong, while I put on more lipstick. Don't you dare let him in until I say so.'

She snatched off her apron, raced to her dressing-table, and disappeared in a cloud of powder while Pongwiffy went to answer the door.

Outside stood Ronald in all his glory. Hat of Knowledge, Robe of Mystery, Mystic Staff, Cloak of Darkness, the lot. In fact, he looked exactly the same as he did when we last saw him, except that his spots were worse. (This usually happened with

Sharkadder's beauty preparations, which were very hit and miss, with invariably nasty side-effects. In other words, they might clear your spots, but in doing so they'd give you a terrible rash.)

'Oh,' said Ronald heavily. 'It's you, Pongwiffy. I didn't know you were invited.'

'Well, I am, so there,' said Pongwiffy with satisfaction. 'Spotty,' she added in an undertone. She and Ronald had never liked each other.

'Come in, Ronald, come in!' trilled Sharkadder from inside. 'Whatever are you thinking of, Pong, keeping Ronald waiting on the doorstep!'

'You might as well give me your cloak, then,' said Pongwiffy, deceptively casual. 'I'll hang it up for you.'

'No, thank you,' said Ronald, pushing past. 'It's new. I don't want you touching it.'

'You'll be hot,' Pongwiffy warned him. 'It's really boiling in there. She's been cooking all afternoon, it's like an oven. You'll be much more comfortable with your cloak off.'

'Since when did you care for my comfort?' asked Ronald suspiciously. 'Anyway, a Wizard and his Cloak of Darkness are Never Parted. Except behind the secret portals of the Wizards' Club. And when we're in bed. I thought you would have known that, Pongwiffy. By the way, is that a Hamster on your hat? And has it got a stupid accent, by any chance?'

'It is,' said Hugo, bristling. 'It has. Vat of it?'

'Aha! I knew it! I've been hearing all about you! King Futtout's been complaining about you, if you must know. I might have known it'd be something to do with you, Pongwiffy . . .'

At this point, Ronald was interrupted, as Sharkadder swooped down upon him with glad cries and attempted to smother him in lipsticky kisses.

'Please, Aunt Sharkadder,' protested Ronald, wriggling out of her embrace, smoothing down his robe and straightening his hat, which had been knocked crooked. 'Please. Do you mind . . . the robes . . .'

'Oh, but look at you!' cried Sharkadder fondly, fussing around and picking imaginary bits of cotton from his shoulder. 'Look at you in all your fancy finery! When I think I used to dandle you on my lap and conjure up little green explosions to make you cry. Little did I know you'd grow into such a tall, handsome young man. Of course, good looks run in the family. Pity about the spots, though. Didn't you use that new cream I sent you?'

'Can we have tea now?' asked Pongwiffy from the tea-table, through a mouthful of custard. 'I don't know about anyone else, but I'm starving.'

'Me too,' announced Hugo, from somewhere inside the dish of green jelly.

'Badness me, whatever am I thinking of? Where are my manners?' cried Sharkadder. 'Sit down, Ronald, do. Pongwiffy, get your fist out of that trifle and pull Ronald up a chair. Then we can sit down and have tea and Ronald can tell us all about his interview at the Palace.'

And she ran to turn the kettle off.

'Nice cloak,' remarked Pongwiffy. 'I like the stars on the lining. Very smart. What, glued on are they? Or sewn?'

'I really have no idea,' said Ronald.

'You'd better take it off if you're having tea. It being so new and all,' remarked Pongwiffy helpfully.

'No, thank you,' said Ronald. 'I told you before. I don't want to take it off.'

'You might spill something down your front,' said Pongwiffy.

'No, I won't,' said Ronald, staring at her.

'*I* might spill something down your front,' threatened Pongwiffy.

At that point, Sharkadder came hastening back with the teapot.

'Right, shall I be mother? Now, do help yourself to a sandwich, Ronald. There's spiderspread, grasshopper in mayonnaise or slug and lettuce. I've cut the crusts off. Here's your tea. Strong with three sugars in a proper cup and saucer, just how you like it.'

'Where's *my* tea?' complained Pongwiffy.

'It's coming, it's coming, just wait. I do hope everything's to your liking, Ronald. I'm afraid it won't be up to the standard of the meals you get at the Wizards' Club.'

'Oh absolutely,' agreed Ronald. 'Some pretty amazing spreads we get there, I can tell you. Three courses at least. And paper serviettes.'

'You hear that, Pong?' breathed Sharkadder, terribly impressed. 'Three courses! And paper serviettes. Well I never.'

'Oh yes,' said Ronald, warming to his theme. 'Three courses and a clean table-cloth every day. And our own goblets with our names on.'

'Clean table-cloths!' breathed Sharkadder enthralled. 'Own goblets! So sophisticated! Imagine, Pongwiffy.'

'So what?' growled Pongwiffy. 'So what if there are clean table-cloths? Who cares? I hate clean table-cloths. Don't encourage him, Sharkadder.'

Sharkadder ignored her.

'You know what I'm dying to hear about, Ronald?' she trilled, and gave a girlish little skip. 'The password! Tell us about the password, do! It's too, too thrilling!'

Ronald shook his head.

'Sorry,' he said importantly. 'No can do, Aunt. All very hush-hush. Only Us Wizards know it.'

'It's probably something really stupid and obvious, like Open Sesame,' said Pongwiffy.

Ronald gasped.

'How do you know?' he cried, then went bright red and clapped his hand to his mouth.

'Because you Wizards have no imagination,' explained Pongwiffy.

'Well, I'd sooner you didn't mention it,' Ronald muttered. 'As I said, only Us Wizards are supposed to know it. And the servants, of course.'

'Servants? You have servants up at the Wizards' Club?' said Pongwiffy, suddenly perking up.

'Certainly. Cooks. Butlers. Waiters,' Ronald told her loftily.

'You mean someone else washes your dirty socks?' Pongwiffy wanted to know.

'Of course,' said Ronald. 'We Wizards don't have time to do all the menial tasks. Especially Those Of Us With Proper Jobs,' he added proudly.

'Oh, Ronald!' cried Sharkadder, thrilled to pieces. 'You did it! You got the job up at the Palace! Oh, you clever, clever boy! Tell us all about it, then. How much does it pay? How many weeks holiday? Are there banquet vouchers? What was the Queen wearing? What are your duties?'

'Well – actually, I was about to come to that,' said Ronald. 'There's something I wanted to discuss with you, Aunt. A small favour.'

'Oh yes?' said Sharkadder. She was still smiling a wide, toothy smile, but her voice bore a hint of frost. She was suspicious of people who asked favours, as anyone who knows Pongwiffy has a right to be. 'And what might that be, Ronald?'

'Well, King Futtout tells me there have been . . . well, a few problems with you Witches lately. I'm afraid he's rather upset. And quite frankly, Aunt, it's got to stop.'

There was a long pause, during which Sharkadder and Pongwiffy looked at Ronald. Even Hugo stuck his head up over the jelly dish and treated him to a long, hard stare.

'Problems, Ronald?' said Sharkadder in a silky voice. 'What sort of problems?'

'Oh, you know. Bat-droppings on the lawn. Unlawful use of the swimming-pool. Er – some unfortunate business with the Princess – er . . .'

Ronald trailed off. Suddenly he began to feel a little uncertain.

'So?' asked Sharkadder. 'That's Witch Business. I wouldn't like to think that you were interfering in Witch Business, Ronald.'

'Quite right, Sharky,' chipped in Pongwiffy. 'You tell him. It's bad luck to stick your nose in Witch Business. I'd have thought you'd have known that, Ronald. All those exams.'

'I just thought, you know . . . maybe a few words in the right ear . . .'

At this point, Ronald's confidence deserted him completely. His throat went dry and he badly wanted a drink. He lifted the brimming cup to his lips and attempted to take a sip.

It was then that Pongwiffy leaned across the table

and violently joggled his elbow, crying, 'Ronald! You've just spilt some tea on your lovely new cloak! Take it off immediately, I'll get a cloth!'

'Oh, Pongwiffy, how could you be so clumsy!' wailed Sharkadder, leaping forward and dabbing violently at Ronald with the first thing that came to hand, which happened to be the blanket from Dudley's basket. So enthusiastic was she that Ronald toppled backwards out of his chair and landed on the floor with a little scream.

Just to complicate things still further, Dudley chose that very moment to stage his return. He

came leaping in through the window and came face to face with his old enemy Hugo, who, by way of greeting, stuck his tongue out and flicked a spoonful of frog jelly in Dudley's one remaining eye. An interesting chase followed, resulting in a lot of food ending up on Sharkadder's newly spring-cleaned floor.

Meanwhile, under the table, Ronald fended off Pongwiffy as she attempted to forcibly divest him of his cloak. She would have succeeded too, if Sharkadder hadn't come to the rescue.

It is best to pull a veil over the rest of the proceedings and skip straight to the outcome. The outcome was that Pongwiffy and Hugo got thrown out of the tea-party in disgrace. Once again,

Pongwiffy was minus a best friend. She didn't even get one star from the cloak of darkness, let alone seven.

But she did get a good tea.

And an idea.

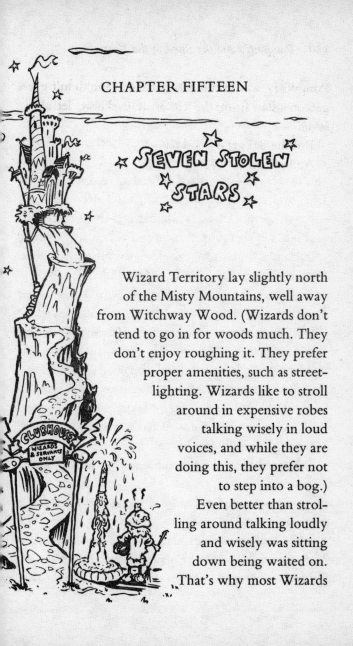

CHAPTER FIFTEEN

SEVEN STOLEN STARS

Wizard Territory lay slightly north
of the Misty Mountains, well away
from Witchway Wood. (Wizards don't
tend to go in for woods much. They
don't enjoy roughing it. They prefer
proper amenities, such as street-
lighting. Wizards like to stroll
around in expensive robes
talking wisely in loud
voices, and while they are
doing this, they prefer not
to step into a bog.)
Even better than strol-
ling around talking loudly
and wisely was sitting
down being waited on.
That's why most Wizards

tended to live at the Clubhouse. The Clubhouse was, as you might expect, very posh indeed. It sat proudly glittering on the top of a very exclusive hill at the end of an imposing driveway consisting of yellow and pink crazy paving with silver grouting. The Wizards' flag (a sort of messy mishmash of crossed staves and lightning bolts and stars and moons and stuff) flew from the topmost turret. There were curly bits and twiddly bits and bits which squirted coloured water. There were spirals and murals and gargoyles and symbols. Someone had gone mad with a lot of gold paint.

'So *that's* the famous Wizards' Clubhouse,' said Pongwiffy, peering around an ornamental fountain. 'Don't think much of it, do you? Give me a nice filthy hovel any time. All those fancy spires and portals and stars and carved knockers and stuff. Bad taste, I call it.'

'Ssh,' hissed Hugo. 'Keep voice down.'

'And the colours! Yuck. Makes my eyes water. All that pink and gold. What's wrong with nice plain serviceable black, I want to know?'

'Mistress! Please!' begged Hugo. 'Ve don't vant to be catched.'

'Oh, stop being such an old worry-pouches. If I'd known you were going to be like this I wouldn't have brought you with me. Where's all that famous Hamster swashbuckle you're always talking about? Where's your sense of adventure? All that spring-cleaning's turned you soft. Now, where's my disguise?'

Obediently the Broom came scuttling forward with a badly-wrapped newspaper parcel.

'I still say you crazy,' said Hugo in a sulky voice. He didn't like being called soft. 'If Sourmuddle find out about zis, she throw you out of Coven. Zen I out of job.'

'Serve you right,' said Pongwiffy. 'In fact, just recently, I've been wondering if you're up to the job. It seems that if I want anything done I have to do it myself. Anyway, it's taken me ages to get all the ingredients together and I'm not stopping now. I've only got the seven stars to go. If all goes well, we can do it tonight. Now, how do I look?'

Hugo looked at her. Slowly, he shook his head. 'It von't vork,' he said.

'Yes it will. I am the very image of a rosy-cheeked washerwoman.'

'No you not,' argued Hugo. 'Vashervimmin always clean. You filthy.'

'But I've got the frilly apron and the cap and everything!' Pongwiffy was hurt. She had indeed gone to a lot of trouble to look the part, even making sure that a handful of clothes-pegs and an old bar of soap (stolen, naturally) protruded from her apron pocket.

'Zey filthy too. I tell you it von't vork.'

'Well, who's fault is all this anyway!' cried Pong-wiffy crossly, stamping her foot. 'If you hadn't thrown out my Cardigan of Invisibility, we wouldn't have to bother with all this disguise nonsense!'

'I not throw it out!' denied Hugo.

'Oh ha! Next thing you'll be saying you didn't even see it!'

'Of course I not see it! How I see it? It invisible!'

'Oh, pass the laundry-basket. I'm not standing around here arguing with you a minute longer! I'll show you how it's done. Stay here and keep watch with the Broom. And be prepared for a quick get-away.'

Bad-temperedly, Pongwiffy snatched up her most important prop – the battered red plastic basket she had found on the rubbish tip – and marched up the crazy-paving path which led to the star-studded front doors of the Wizards' Club.

'Not zat one! Not ze front door! Go to ze tradesman's entrance at ze side!' called Hugo. But he was too late. Pongwiffy had already knocked, using the heavy carved knocker. Not content with that, she gave the bell-rope a determined yank and at the same time kicked the door sharply with the toe of her boot.

'Open up,' bawled Pongwiffy over the clanging. 'Hurry up in there, get a move on!'

'She blow it!' moaned Hugo to the Broom. 'I know it! She blow it! She over-confident. I not look.'

Pongwiffy tapped her foot impatiently. She was just about to kick the door again, when there came an unpleasant crackling noise from one of the decorative stars. Pongwiffy gave a little jump. Then:

'This is a recorded message,' shrieked a harsh voice in Pongwiffy's ear. 'Oozat? Wachoo want? Please speak clearly after the tone or belt up and go away.'

There was a terrible burst of static, then silence.

'Washerwoman,' bellowed Pongwiffy into the star. 'Harmless old washerwoman, come to collect the dirty clothes.'

Immediately, she came up in green spots.

'Password?' grated the voice.

'Open Sesame, of course,' squawked Pongwiffy. 'Hurry up, I haven't got all day. I've got to get back to my – er – mangle. Oh yes, there's a mountain of ironing I've got to do. That's because I'm a washer-woman.'

There was a pause, followed by a great deal of interference from the primitive intercom. (Wizards are creative types. When it comes to anything the slightest bit technical, they're all thumbs.) Then, slowly and dramatically, with a good deal of theatrical squeaking, the doors swung open and Pongwiffy strode into the vestibule.

Inside, it had been done out in red flock wallpaper. A turgid organ version of Magic Moments issued forth tinnily from a couple of cheap wall speakers. Dull portraits of miserable-looking bearded ancients in pointy hats stared down from the walls. There was a headache-inducing, swirling, multi-coloured carpet. There was a polished desk marked RECEPTION behind which a bored-looking female Zombie with large brass ear-rings and a tangled mass of green hair chewed gum and read a magazine.

Pongwiffy marched over to the reception desk and briskly rang the bell.

'Yeah?' said the Zombie, not even looking up. She was reading an article entitled, 'Scott Sinister – Man or Myth?'

'Where's the cloakroom?' said Pongwiffy. 'Dearie.'

Slowly, the Zombie looked up and stared rudely. Pongwiffy gave her what she imagined to be a broad Honest Washerwoman smile and hummed a snatch of 'I'm Forever Blowing Bubbles'.

'Oooja saya wuzagin?' said the Zombie. She wore a badge proclaiming that she was Brenda and that she was At Your Service.

'Harmless old washerwoman. Mrs Flushing's my name. From the new laundry down the road,' said Pongwiffy.

'Nobody's said nuffink to me,' said Brenda, pulling her gum out to arm's length in a long grey string then letting it coil back down into her mouth.

'You mean they haven't told you?' cried Pongwiffy. 'About the new arrangement? How I'm to come and collect the dirty cloaks every Wednesday? Well, if that doesn't beat all. You'd think they'd have told you. You're not expecting me, then?'

'No,' said Brenda, blowing a bubble. ''Ere. You're covered in green spots, you are.'

'Oh, am I? Really? Probably my allergy. I'm allergic to multi-coloured carpets. Frightened by one as a child. Terrible thing. Oh well, can't stand chatting here all day. This way, is it? To the little boys' room? Down this passage?'

''Ere, jussa minute, you can't . . .'

'Don't worry, dear, I'll find it.'

And Pongwiffy marched purposefully off down a long passageway, leaving Brenda with an uncertain expression on her face.

★

The lounge was packed with Wizards. For the most part, they sat silently in overstuffed armchairs, smoking cigars, glancing impatiently at their watches, snoozing, doing the crossword, leafing through back copies of *Wizards' World* or merely dribbling into their beards whilst waiting for the dinner gong.

It was hard to know they were Wizards when they were without their Hats of Knowledge and Cloaks of Darkness. Bald heads and very old woolly jumpers predominated. An ancient retainer with a paper bag over his head(?) creaked around amongst them, handing out small smoking glasses of green stuff.

Ronald was standing casually at the window, pretending not to mind that all the chairs had been taken so there was nowhere for him to sit. Neither had there been a peg available in the cloakroom. He was the new boy, so everyone tended to ignore him. He was, he noticed, the only one who hadn't been offered a glass of the smoking green stuff.

'Hasn't our Brenda got round to ordering a chair for you yet, young Ronald?' jeered a rat-faced Wizard, from the depths of the comfiest sofa. His name was Frank the Foreteller and he specialized in Foreknowledge.

'Actually, I rather like standing,' said Ronald.

'I knew you were going to say that,' cried Frank the Foreteller triumphantly, slapping his knee. 'I

knew he was going to say that,' he repeated to the
room at large. Several Wizards looked up from their
newspapers and stared at Ronald as though they
were seeing him for the first time.

'You're looking flushed, young Ronald. Why
don't you take your cloak off?' suggested Frank the
Foreteller, winking at the watching Wizards, really
rubbing things in. 'We're all informal here, lad, you
don't have to stand on ceremony.'

'Actually, I don't have a peg,' said Ronald stiffly.

'I know you don't,' crowed Frank the Foreteller.
'And I can foretell you won't have one for a long
time to come,' he added spitefully.

'Oh,' said Ronald. There didn't seem much else
he could add.

'And how did the interview go, young Ronald?
Applied for a post at the Palace, eh?' sneered Frank
the Foreteller.

'Well, yes, I . . .'

'Don't tell me, don't tell me, you got the job. I knew that. Saw it in the tea-leaves yesterday. So old Futtout wants you to do something about the Witches, eh?'

'Well, I . . .'

'Yes, yes, I know, you don't have to tell me. Of course, you know you've bitten off more than you can chew, don't you?'

'I don't think I . . .'

'Oh yes, oh dear me yes. Tricky business, dealing with Witches. You're going to come a cropper.'

'King Futtout has every conf – '

'Yes, when it comes to handling Witches, some have got it and some haven't.'

'Look, I really . . .'

'No point in arguing, young feller, I know. I can foretell. I can foretell most things. In fact, I can foretell the dinner gong's about to go.'

There really was no point in talking to him. Ronald turned away. As he did so, he caught a glimpse of someone – a servant, no doubt – hurrying past the doorway carrying what looked like a heaped pile of clothes in a basket. For a moment, there was an unpleasant, somehow familiar smell in the air. He couldn't quite place it, but he knew he'd smelt it before. It was on the tip of his nose . . .

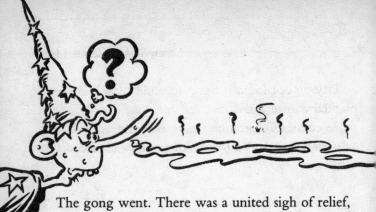

The gong went. There was a united sigh of relief, and a general stirring and cracking of bones as the Wizards heaved themselves out of their armchairs and made for the door, eager to be first in the queue for the dining-room.

The exodus was halted by the sudden appearance of Brenda in the doorway. She was breathing heavily and rather flushed, as though she had been lumbering a shade faster than usual.

'You kin orl siddown again,' announced Brenda. 'That weren't the dinner gong. Dinner ain't ready yet. That were the emergency gong. I just come up to tell you we bin robbed, see? Loada cloaks gawn from the cloakroom. An' before you start, it weren't my fault. She said she wuz a washerwoman. 'Ow wuz I to know?'

There was instant panic amongst the Wizards. This was grave news indeed! Not only were the cloaks stolen, dinner wasn't ready!

Ronald couldn't resist it. He turned to Frank the Foreteller.

'Pity you couldn't have foretold that,' he remarked with a smirk.

He could afford to be smug, You see, *he was the only one who hadn't hung his cloak up in the cloakroom!*

CHAPTER SIXTEEN

It was full moon – or, as Granny Malodour would have put it, Fulle Moone. In the hovel, preparations were well under way. The fire was lit and the cauldron was giving off promising gloppy sort of noises. Rich, brown, muddy fumes curled into the air, mingling unpleasantly with the all-pervading smell of Reeka Reeka Roses. Pongwiffy peered in at the brew, sniffed, stirred, tasted and gave a nod.

'The quicksand's nearly ready. How are you getting on with the chopping?'

'I done ze visker and ze fezzer and ze golden hair. I still got ze bobble and ze stars to do.'

'Well, get a move on,' snapped Pongwiffy. 'We've only got until the cock crows, you know.'

'Chop, chop, chop, all I do is chop. It make my paw ache. I sink it my turn to stir now.'

'Certainly not! Haven't you heard the old saying? Too Many Witches Spoil The Brew. Familiars chop, Witches stir. That's the way things are done. Keep chopping or you're fired.'

Grumpily, she hunched down in her chair, bit her nails and scowled around. It wasn't like her to be so bad-tempered when she was brewing up. It was just that, somehow, things didn't *feel* right. There simply wasn't an atmosphere. Everywhere was too clean and tidy. There were too few shadows; there was far too much hygiene. Even the cauldron had been scraped out and there were none of those interesting little black bits to drop into whatever was cooking.

Pongwiffy sighed deeply. She missed the dirt and the cobwebs and the little black bits. In the past there had always been dirt and cobwebs and little black bits when she made a brew. There was *supposed* to be dirt and cobwebs and little black bits. It was traditional.

'If you only let me use uzzer paw . . .'

'No.'

Firmly, Pongwiffy tapped Granny Malodour's spell book. which lay crumbling away before her on the kitchen table.

'No. The recipe says Using Thy Left Hand Only. We've got to do it right. The important thing about making a decent brew is to get the details right.'

'Vy ze Broom not help?' sulked Hugo.

'Because I've posted it outside on guard duty. I've told it to give three loud knocks as a warning signal if anyone comes. We don't want unexpected visitors, do we?'

'Hmm. I just hope all zis choppink verth it,' said Hugo doubtfully. 'Suppose it not verk? Sometimes zese old recipes . . .'

'You just don't understand, do you? This is Granny's *Wishing Water*, Hugo. Granny's spells *always* work. And if it doesn't, I shall blame you. It'll be because the lock of hair isn't fresh . . .'

She broke off as there came three thunderous knocks on the door. Hugo jumped six inches into the air and the knife he was holding dropped from

numb paws. Quite a bit of chopped hair spilt on the
floor. Guiltily, Pongwiffy snatched up the cauldron
lid and slammed it down over the illicit brew.

'It her!' gasped Hugo. 'It Sourmuddle! Now you
done it! She caught us! Now vat ve gonna do?'

'Stall her,' hissed Pongwiffy, throwing Granny
Malodour's spell book under the nearest cushion and
spraying the air liberally with Reeka Reeka Roses.

Then a voice spoke.

'Pong?' it said. 'Is that you
in there, Pong? It's all right,
you can open up. It's only me,
Sharky.'

Gasping with relief, Pongwiffy scuttled across and threw
open the hovel door. Sure
enough, outside stood Sharkadder. She had obviously flown
here in a hurry, because her
Broomstick looked all in. In
one hand she held her handbag.
In the other was a large, fragrant,
still-warm, home-made fungus sponge. Pongwiffy's
Broom stood on the doorstep, twiggy arms out-
stretched, boldly blocking her way.

'Hello, Pong,' said Sharkadder, holding out the
sponge. 'Tell your idiot Broomstick to get out of

my way, will you? I've brought you a cake as a peace-offering. Just out of the oven.'

'Sharky! What a sight for sore eyes! Come in, come in!' cried Pongwiffy, never one to turn down an offer of friendship. Or cake, for that matter. 'I just can't tell you how pleased I am to see you. Broom! Get out of Witch Sharkadder's way this minute!'

Huffily, the Broom moved to one side and threw itself against the hovel wall. Sharkadder propped hers next to it, and the two of them began the low, mutinous rustling which is the Broom equivalent of discontented whispering.

'Come on in then,' said Pongwiffy, reaching for the sponge. 'I suppose you've come to make up?'

'No, I made up before I came,' explained Sharkadder, following her in. 'Doesn't it show?'

It did. Her hair was frizzed, her face was chalky white, she was wearing her longest spiderleg eyelashes and a great deal of beetroot-coloured lipstick.

'But if you mean have I come to make friends again, yes I have,' she added. 'I've decided to forgive you again, Pong. I've been talking it over with Dudley, and I've come to the conclusion that Ronald was every bit as much to blame as you for spoiling my tea-party.'

'Oh yes?' said Pongwiffy, biting into the fungus

sponge. 'And Dudley? What conclusion did he come to?'

'The opposite,' confessed Sharkadder. 'He says it's all your fault. I must admit I agreed with him. Until Ronald sent me a *dry-cleaning bill*!'

'Never!' cried Pongwiffy. 'And you his aunty? Surely not!'

'Yes, he did. The cheek of it. It arrived this morning. And there was me thinking it was a letter saying thank you for the lovely tea. And not a word about the spot cream I gave him either. No manners at all.'

'I told you so,' Pongwiffy reminded her. 'If that's not a typical Wizard. I always said Ronald was a snobby little swankpot, didn't I?'

'And you were right. My badness, it's clean in here, isn't it?' Sharkadder suddenly exclaimed. 'I do believe you've swept the floor! And all your cobwebs have gone. It doesn't look like your hovel at all, Pongwiffy.'

'I know,' said Pongwiffy, with a bitter little glance at Hugo, who sucked in his pouches and looked obstinate.

'Anyway, as I told Dudley, "Friendship's Thicker Than Bogwater," I said. Besides, I know you're up to something and I want to know what it is.'

Sharkadder's long white nose sniffed the air.

'Aha! I thought so! I detect hot quicksand. You're working on your secret spell, aren't you? Is that a brew you've got going over there in the cauldron? Let's have a look.'

Sharkadder swept across, lifted the cauldron lid and examined the bubbling quicksand with a critical eye.

'Smells awful. Is Dudley's whisker in there?' she asked.

'Not yet.'

'Hmm. There's none of your usual little black bits,' observed Sharkadder. 'What is it, anyway?' she added. 'Come on, Pong, you might as well come clean.'

'Come clean? Me? Never!' said Pongwiffy with a shudder. 'But I suppose now you're here and we're friends again, I might as well tell you everything. Keep your eye on the cauldron while I put the kettle on. Hugo! What did I just tell you? Get on with that chopping.'

And while Hugo got on with the chopping, Sharkadder stirred the cauldron and drank bogwater and Pongwiffy ate the sponge and showed her Granny Malodour's recipe and told her all about the difficulties she'd had getting hold of the ingredients.

'Well!' said Sharkadder, when she had finished. 'Well, I never did. So *that's* what it's all about! You've got the recipe for Granny Malodour's famous Wishing Water! Well, well, well. Lucky old you. I've always wanted to try that stuff. You should have told me that's what you were planning, Pongwiffy. I'd have pulled out one of Dudley's whiskers myself. And if it comes out right, you mean to enter it for the Spell of the Year Competition, did you say?'

'Most definitely,' agreed Pongwiffy. 'So you see why I wanted to keep it a secret?'

'I suppose so,' said Sharkadder doubtfully. 'Although I still think you could have told *me* about it. After all, I am your best friend.'

'You didn't want me to come in,' Pongwiffy reminded her. 'You wanted to get on with the spring-cleaning, remember? You said you didn't want me smelling the place up.'

Sharkadder looked sheepish.

'You caught me at a bad moment,' she confessed.

'Not to worry. I forgive you,' said Pongwiffy graciously. 'And I tell you what!' she added, in a spirit of generosity. 'You can help me! We'll do it together, and we'll both enter it for the competition. It'll be a joint entry. Pongwiffy and Sharkadder's

Wonderful Wishing Water. It's got a certain ring to it, don't you think?'

Sharkadder thought about it. She'd been far too busy spring-cleaning to give much thought to the Spell of the Year Competition. She had vaguely thought about entering her new spot cream, the one she'd tried out on Ronald, but looking at him she suspected it still needed a bit of work. That was the trouble with spring-cleaning. It left no time for Magic.

'Think of the prizes,' Pongwiffy tempted her.

Sharkadder thought of the prizes. There were some good ones. A large silver cup with your name on, for a start. Plus a year's interest-free credit at Malpractiss Magic Inc., two carefree weeks in the drizzle at Sludgehaven-on-Sea, time-share on a flying carpet, a year's subscription for the *Daily Miracle* and, for some strange reason, a lifetime's supply of Reeka Reeka Roses.

'We're sure to win,' said Pongwiffy confidently. 'Besides, I'm really looking forward to trying Granny's Wishing Water again. I tell you, Sharky, this stuff is Magic! It really works. One sip, one wish. Simple as that. Imagine, Sharky. Your heart's secret desire.'

Sharkadder had a fleeting day-dream for a moment that involved a small, exclusive dress shop in a better part of the wood and a career in model-ling.

'All right then,' said Sharkadder. 'What can I do to help?'

'Chop,' said Pongwiffy and Hugo together.

CHAPTER SEVENTEEN

'Who did you say you were again?' said Sourmuddle snappily, fumbling for her glasses. She was standing on her doorstep in her nighty in the drizzle in the dark at a stupid hour of the night while some pushy, pimpled pest in a pointy hat shouted down her ear-trumpet, and she didn't take kindly to it.

'RONALD! I'M RONALD!'

'Well, Donald, let's just get one thing clear before I catch my death. I don't want double glazing or patio doors or a cheap ironing-board cover or a selection of alpine scenes hand-painted on velvet. Neither do I want my garden weeding or my windows washing or my chimney swept. What I *do* want, Roland, is a decent night's sleep. So why don't you just run along before I lose my temper and turn you into something nasty?'

'I'M NOT SELLING ANYTHING!' bellowed Ronald. 'I'M A WIZARD.'

'A what?'

'A WIZARD!'

'Here,' said Grandwitch Sourmuddle, polishing her glasses with the end of her nightcap. 'Here, you remind me of someone, you know.'

'I'M RONALD! SHARKADDER'S MY AUNT!'

'Wait a minute, wait a minute, it's on the tip of my – ha! I know who it is! Sharkadder's awful little nephew! The stuck-up one with the pimples. The one who wants to be a Wizard when he grows up. Rudolph or something. You're the spitting image.'

'RONALD!' screamed Ronald through tortured tonsils. 'RONALD! IT'S ME! I *HAVE* GROWN UP. I *AM* A WIZARD AND I'M HERE ON OFFICIAL BUSINESS! I WISH TO MAKE A FORMAL COMPLAINT ABOUT ONE OF YOUR WITCHES!'

'Complaint? What have you got to complain about? You're not standing on your doorstep in your night-shirt, are you? If anyone's got a complaint, it's me. And stop shouting like that, you're giving me a headache. Think I'm deaf or something?'

'IT'S ABOUT – it's about Pongwiffy, Grandwitch

Sourmuddle. She's really overstepped the mark this time.'

'Eh? Pongwiffy? What about Pongwiffy? If you're referring to that Princess Business, young Randolph, I've already dealt with that. I've told her to write to the Palace and apologize.'

'No, no, it's much worse than that. Earlier today, cunningly disguised as a washerwoman, she infiltrated Us Wizards' private Clubhouse and stole a number of cloaks. These were later retrieved from the bottom of an ornamental fountain. Upon examination, we found that several valuable stars have been forcibly removed from the linings. The owners will, of course, be claiming compensation.'

'Hold your horses, sonny,' snapped Sourmuddle. 'Are you quite sure about this? You're making a serious allegation, you know.'

'Absolutely,' agreed Ronald eagerly. 'I'm glad you see it our way, Sourmuddle. Stealing Wizards' cloaks is a serious business.'

'The cloaks? Who gives a bat squeak for the cloaks? No, what I'm annoyed about is that I personally banned Pongwiffy from all Magical activity for one entire week. She's not allowed to read so much as one tea-leaf. Are you saying she's still running about making a nuisance of herself? In defiance of my orders?'

'Yes,' said Ronald, nodding vigorously. 'Yes, that's exactly what she is doing. Absolutely.'

'Wait there on the doorstep while I get my dressing-gown,' ordered Sourmuddle. 'And don't touch anything. I don't trust you Wizards.'

'Can't I come in? It's drizzling.'

Sourmuddle's answer was to shut the door firmly in his face. Ronald turned his collar up, shuffled about on the step and allowed himself a little smile. Despite the weather, for once, things were going quite well.

CHAPTER EIGHTEEN

CAUGHT IN THE ACT

Things were also going quite well at Number One, Dump Edge. All the ingredients had been added to the brew, which was now bubbling nicely and giving off gratifyingly black, oily fumes.

'Mmm. There's something *about* the smell of skunk stock,' said Pongwiffy, sniffing appreciatively and throwing in a cupful of frog-spawn. 'Grab another handful of those fly-droppings, Hugo. I like a nice bit of seasoning. Right, Sharky, what's next?'

'Sit with thy nose pointing due north and thy boots on ye wrong feet,' read Sharkadder. 'Recite thou ye following chant . . .'

'Wait, wait, which way's north?'

'That way,' said Sharkadder and Hugo, simultaneously pointing in opposite directions. At this point, both Brooms had to be brought in and consulted. (Brooms have a kind of inbuilt compass, which is situated approximately half-way up their sticks. They might not know much, but, by golly, they know north.)

It was very soon established that Pongwiffy had to sit looking out the newly-glazed window overlooking her beloved rubbish tip. The tip had swollen considerably, mainly because the piles of junk that Hugo and the Broom had removed from the hovel had finally been returned to their rightful place. Pongwiffy sighed as she looked out over it, wiped away a nostalgic tear then concentrated on the business in hand.

'Right, I've swopped my boots round. Where's the chant? Pass me Granny's spell book, Sharky. Hurry up, it's nearly dawn and my feet are killing me.'

'Why have I got to do all the menial tasks?' grumbled Sharkadder, whose arm ached from chopping. 'Why can't I do the chant?'

But she did as she was told.

'Right,' said Pongwiffy. 'Here goes. Leap around the cauldron, all of you. Brooms included.'

'Where does it say that?' Sharkadder wanted to know. 'Where in that spell does it say we have to leap?'

'It doesn't. I just think it adds to the atmosphere, don't you? Just stop whining and do it, all right?'

Sighing, Sharkadder gave a small leap and waved her long arms around. Hugo did a spirited tap-dance and the two Brooms hopped about obligingly, in a better mood now they had been consulted about north. Pongwiffy waited a moment or two to let them all get into the swing of the thing, then began to chant in her best, professional cackling voice:

> *'Snap and crackle, scream and cackle,*
> *Can't catch cows with fishing-tackle.*
> *Bubble, brew, the way thou oughter,*
> *Then turn into Wishing Water!'*

She signalled the dancers to halt. Puffing a bit, they jogged to a stop and listened. Nothing happened.

'Where's the cock-crow?' said Pongwiffy with a worried frown. 'The cock's supposed to crow.'

'Keep going,' panted Hugo. 'Say it again. You supposed to continue ze chantink.'

'It'd better work this time,' said Sharkadder with a sniff. 'I'm not leaping much more, I tell you. These shoes aren't made for leaping.'

> *'Snap and crackle, scream and cackle,*
> *Can't catch cows with fishing-tackle.*
> *Bubble, brew, the way thou . . .'*

That did it. The brew gave a convulsive heave and boiled over. Where the brew met the fire, the

flames turned green and blazed up dramatically.

'Vow!' said Hugo. 'Zat amazink!'

There was a hissing and a fizzling and a spluttering and puffs of lime green smoke. Little crackles of shocking-pink lightning arced above the cauldron. The startled cauldron-dancers drew back in alarm as pink and green sparks rained down and Pongwiffy hastily reached for a jug of flowers, just in case. There was an eye-watering, multi-coloured eruption of light –

And then, far away, the cock crew. Five times. Just like it was supposed to do. And with the first crow, the miniature firework display above the cauldron fizzled out, leaving an unappetizing purplish liquid simmering sluggishly in the bottom.

Pongwiffy peered in and gave a deep sniff. Then: 'That's it!' she said excitedly. 'Wishing Water! It's come out just the way I remember it! Colour, smell, everything! This is the moment we've been waiting for. Hugo, fetch me the ladle. I'm having first taste.'

'Oh no you're not, Pongwiffy,' said a voice from the doorway. It was accompanied by a theatrical rumble of thunder.

Everyone turned round. There stood Sourmuddle in fluffy tartan slippers and a quilted blue dressing-gown that had seen better days. Behind her stood Snoop, rubbing his eyes and looking like he'd just woken up. And behind *him* stood Ronald, wearing a malicious little smile.

'Oh, Sourmuddle, it's you,' said Pongwiffy with

a gulp. 'What a lovely surprise. Just in time to sample my new brew.'

'I'll take charge of that,' said Sourmuddle sternly. 'Making Magic behind my back indeed! After I've banned you! And what are you doing here, Sharkadder?'

'Trying to stop her,' explained Sharkadder. 'I wasn't dancing around the cauldron or anything. Oh, dear me, no.'

'Hello, Aunt,' said Ronald with a little smirk.

'Ronald,' said Sharkadder in a voice that could curdle milk. 'Get lost.'

'You know, I'm sure I recognize that smell,' said Sourmuddle, sniffing. 'What is it, anyway?'

'Granny Malodour's Wishing Water,' said Pongwiffy. 'I might as well tell you. You'll find out for yourself in the end anyway.'

'Really?' said Sourmuddle with an interested gleam in her eye. 'Granny Malodour's Wishing Water? The real stuff? You're sure?'

She shuffled over to the cauldron and peered in. Snoop, Sharkadder, Pongwiffy and Hugo clustered round and they all stood over it and stroked their chins, examining the unpleasant goo with professional interest.

'Can I see?' asked Ronald, trying to look over their shoulders.

'No,' said Sourmuddle. 'This is Witch Business. Stand back.'

'Go away, Spotty,' said Pongwiffy.

'And write a nice thank-you letter,' suggested Sharkadder in a voice of steel.

Ronald flinched and stayed where he was.

'You're right, you know,' said Sourmuddle. 'It *is* Wishing Water. Once smelt, never forgotten.'

'The very same,' nodded Pongwiffy. 'Made to Granny's very own recipe, which I just happened to come across. Look. Here's her spell book.'

'Well, well, well,' said Sourmuddle with a little chuckle. 'And I thought Granny Malodour's recipe for Wishing Water was lost for ever.'

'Why? Have you tried it, then, Sourmuddle?' asked Sharkadder curiously.

'Certainly I have. Granny used to send me over a bottle every Hallowe'en. Disgusting taste. But it worked.'

'Why? What did you wish for?' chorused Pongwiffy and Sharkadder together.

'What d'you think? To become Grandwitch, of course. To get to be Mistress of the Coven and boss everybody about. And my wish came true. Which is why I'm ordering you to hurry up and stick that stuff in a bottle because I'm confiscating it right now.'

'Oh, Sourmuddle, please!' wailed Pongwiffy. '*Please* don't do this! Not until you hear about my plan!'

'Plan? What plan?'

'The plan that's going to benefit all of us. You see, I'm planning to enter Granny's Wishing Water for the Spell of the Year Competition. There are some really good prizes this year. I wanted to share them with all my good friends. And bring honour to the Coven, of course.'

'Really?' said Sourmuddle, perking up. 'What, you'd share the holiday and everything?'

'Oh yes. I thought *you* might like to go on that, Sourmuddle, I know how much you like Sludgehaven-on-Sea. And I thought you could keep the silver cup on your mantelpiece, Sourmuddle. It'd look really nice up there.'

There was a long pause.

'It would be nice if a Witch won this year,' Sourmuddle said slowly.

'It would, it certainly would,' agreed Pongwiffy eagerly.

'And I am on the jury . . .' Sourmuddle said thoughtfully.

'I know you are,' said Pongwiffy. 'I know I can count on your vote, Sourmuddle.'

'You mean *we*,' Sharkadder reminded her. 'It's a joint entry, remember?'

'Of course, rules are rules, Pongwiffy, and you'll have to be punished,' added Sourmuddle.

'But not *too* severely,' coaxed Pongwiffy. 'Concentrate, Sourmuddle. Just hold on to that idea of a Witch win. Beating the Wizards. Just think of it.'

'After that idiot with the pigeons up his jumper . . .' said Sourmuddle reflectively.

'You are so right,' said Pongwiffy, shaking her head sadly. 'He never should have got it. We all said so at the time.'

'I'm tempted,' said Sourmuddle. 'What do you think, Snoop?'

'I say,' said Ronald, from somewhere back in the shadows. 'I say, Sourmuddle, look, what about this business of the cloaks and everything? Aren't you going to . . .?'

He trailed off, as would anyone who was being stared at by three Witches, a Demon and a Hamster.

'Just a moment,' said Sourmuddle. 'I wish to consult with Snoop.'

They went into a conspiratorial huddle in the corner, then made up their minds.

'I tell you what, Pongwiffy,' said Sourmuddle briskly. 'We'll compromise. You stick it in a bottle and I'll confiscate it, but you can have it back in time for the Spell of the Year. How about that?'

'All right,' said Pongwiffy with a little sigh. 'But can't we even try it now? Just one sip? Just to make sure it works?'

'Certainly not. You're supposed to be being punished, not getting wishes. You'll just have to wait.'

At that point, Ronald decided to put up a last protest.

'Just a minute,' he croaked feebly. 'I really must protest.'

He really shouldn't have. All he succeeded in doing was drawing attention to himself. To his horror, he was made to hold a bottle at pitchfork point while the disgustingly smelly brew – Wishing Water, as they called it – was poured in. The bottle was a small green demonade bottle with a very narrow neck. Quite a bit

got spilt accidentally on purpose on his robes, he noticed.

'You can go now,' Sourmuddle told him some time later. 'Thank you for your help, young Rodney. Don't want to outstay your welcome, do you? Now, run along, run along. Say goodbye nicely to your aunt. Sharkadder, get rid of him, will you?'

'I'd be delighted,' said Sharkadder. 'Goodbye, Ronald. I'd strongly advise you not to send me another dry-cleaning bill.' She waved her hand casually, and the next thing he knew he was up to his neck in the ornate fountain in the grounds of the Wizards' Club.

'Very nice, Sharkadder, very neat,' said Sourmuddle approvingly when the blue smoke that had been Ronald cleared. She picked up the small green bottle which sat on the floor in the space where he had been.

'Right, I've got the Wishing Water. Don't worry, I'll put it in a safe place. And now, if you'll excuse me, girls, I'm off to get a bit of shut-eye. See you in the morning, Pongwiffy. When you come to clean my boots. Come on, Snoop.'

And with that, she was gone. There wasn't even a puff of smoke.

'See that?' said Sharkadder admiringly. 'Not even any smoke. No wonder she's Grandwitch. Sometimes I think she can see what we're up to from miles away. Hear us talking.'

''Course not,' said Pongwiffy scornfully. 'She's not *that* good. And I wouldn't mind betting she has a swig of that Wishing Water when she gets home.'

'I heard that,' said Sourmuddle's disembodied voice.

'You know what I think?' said Pongwiffy wearily. 'I think it's time for bed. Good night, Sharky. Let yourself out, will you?'

In she climbed. Her boots were still on the wrong feet, but she didn't even notice. She was so tired that she almost didn't mind that the sheets were clean.

CHAPTER NINETEEN

'Your Royal Majesty, Honoured Members of the Judging Panel, Witches, Wizards, Skeletons, Spooks, Ghosts, Ghouls, Zombies, Monsters, Mummies, Demons, Trolls, Vampires, Banshees, Werewolves, Gnomes and last and most definitely least, Goblins – welcome, thrice welcome to the Witchway Hall!' boomed a rich voice from nowhere.

There was an excited buzz as the house lights dimmed. Conversation died away and was replaced by an expectant hush, during which a lone voice shouted out, 'What about us Fiends?'

The heckler was ignored. Instead, there was a rising drum-roll followed by a clash of cymbals, and suddenly a portly Genie in a gaudy red turban and exotic pants materialized stage centre. He was dramatically lit by a single green spotlight, and he was smiling broadly.

'Friends, my name is Ali Pali and I am your Master Of Ceremonies for the evening,' he announced in oily tones and gave a low, sweeping bow.

Pongwiffy knew this particular Genie of old. She gave a start of recognition and clutched Sharkadder's arm.

'It's him again! That Ali Pali! I don't believe it, that Genie gets everywhere! What a nerve he's got. Oi! You! You've got a nerve, you have, Pali!'

'Ssh,' hissed Sharkadder. 'Do you want to spoil our chances?'

'Tonight, O Ladies and Gentlemen,' continued Ali Pali, ignoring them. 'Tonight we see the return of the ever-popular Spell of the Year Competition, sponsored this year by Genie Enterprises, manufacturers of Reeka Reeka Roses, the miracle air-freshener – as used by his gracious Majesty King Futtout II.'

Ali Pali beamed approvingly at King Futtout, who sat miserably in the middle of the Judging Panel. The Judging Panel consisted of six members. They were arranged in a row behind that very same trestle-table which the Witches used for their Emergency Meeting. Tonight it bristled with score-cards, pencils, notepads, water jugs and glasses. On a high shelf nearby was the coveted silver cup.

The front row of the stalls was taken up by hopeful Witch contestants and their Familiars. The second row contained the competing Wizards, who spent a lot of time blowing cigar smoke around and kicking the backs of the seats in front (which we all know is most irritating).

Row Three was occupied by the rest of the contenders who didn't fall into either camp, but who considered themselves no slouches when it came to the old spell-casting. These consisted mostly of assorted Wise men and women, Gypsy Palmists, Tree Demons, Pixies and the Odd Gnome, and they spent most of their time complaining about the double row of tall hats which blocked their view of the stage.

The rest of the seats were occupied by the general public. (Although that's probably too polite a name for them.)

'I trust your Majesty has no objection to my mentioning your royal self in connection with this wonderful product?' Ali Pali added smoothly.

'Erm?' said King Futtout, blushing unhappily. 'Erm . . . no, no, of course not . . . erm.'

'I'm sure we're all very grateful that you could spare us some of your very valuable time, Sire,' crawled Ali Pali, adding heartily, 'Let's have a big hand for his Majesty the King!'

There was a bit of scattered applause and one or two boos. Opinion was divided as to whether or not King Futtout should be on the Judging Panel. After all, he was hardly an expert on Magic. On the other hand, it didn't hurt to keep the local royalty sweet. As Rory pointed out, you never knew when you needed to use the Palace swimming-pool.

For his part, King Futtout would never have come. Spell competitions just weren't his thing. The presence of all those Witches in the audience gave him the willies. He was only there because Beryl and Honeydimple had forced him.

('You tell them,' they had said. 'You tell those Witches they can't get away with it.' And they had said a lot more along the same lines.)

Futtout had rather hoped to forge a sick-note and send along his new Wizard to take his place – but unfortunately, Ronald the Magnificent was himself confined to his turret with a sudden, mysterious cold.

'And now, without more ado, let me introduce the other six members of our esteemed Judging Panel,' continued Ali Pali.

'Firstly, weighing in at two hundred years, we have Grandwitch Sourmuddle, Mistress of the Witch-way Wood Coven!'

As one, the Witches jumped on the seats, threw

their hats in the air, hurled popcorn around and generally misbehaved. Bats zoomed about, stink-bombs were let off, 'Up The Witches' flags were raised, gongs were beaten, Familiars jived in the aisles – it was simply shocking.

'Hooray!'

'Whoopee! You show 'em, Sourmuddle!'

'Attawitch!'

Despite Ali Pali's pleas, Sourmuddle's supporters refused to sit down until their leader put her knitting away, stood up and gave a queenly wave. The non-Witches in the audience sighed and tutted and looked pointedly at their watches.

'And of course, as always, we have the Wizards'

representative, the Venerable Harold the Hood-winker!' announced Ali Pali.

It was now the Wizards' turn to clap and cheer.

'Rah! Rah!' they brayed. 'Good old Harold!'

Nobody else bothered. Harold the Hoodwinker was a permanent fixture on these occasions. The Wizards always wheeled him out because, although he hadn't hoodwinked anyone for years, and slept all the time, he was the oldest club member and entitled to a bit of respect.

'And now, a favourite with all you ladies – Scott Sinister, famous star of stage and screen!'

The tall, thin, pale character in the silly sun-glasses

waved a limp hand, and the audience shouted and clapped enthusiastically. Several of the Banshees in the audience screamed so hard they had to be taken out. A small, bad-tempered Tree Demon brandishing a huge pair of scissors rushed up and demanded an autograph with menaces. Scott Sinister was obviously a popular choice. (Although not with King Futtout, who had at one point nervously asked him to pass down the water jug, only to have the famous star put on the silly sun-glasses and pointedly look the other way.)

'Isn't he lovely?' sighed Pongwiffy to Sharkadder. 'Oh, Scott, Scott! Do you think he'll ever forgive me, Sharky? After that Other Business?'

'No,' said Sharkadder shortly. 'And I'd rather not talk about that Other Business if you don't mind, Pongwiffy.'

(In order to understand the above exchange, you should know that Pongwiffy has had dealings with Scott Sinister before – but that, thankfully, is another story.)

'Have you got the Wishing Water safe?' Pongwiffy asked, staring around uneasily at their fellow competitors. Their fellow competitors stared right back, and several made rude faces and poked their tongues out. 'I don't trust this lot, do you? A right bunch of riff-raff.'

'Of course I've got it. It's in my handbag.'

'I think I ought to have it,' insisted Pongwiffy. 'After all, it's my spell. I found the recipe.'

'Nonsense. Sourmuddle gave it to me to look after. Ssh, he's just about to introduce Pierre.'

'Next, our cookery expert, the very popular Pierre de Gingerbeard!' trumpeted Ali Pali, indicating a genial-looking Dwarf sporting a tall chef's hat and a curling ginger beard.

'Pierre! Bongjoor, Cousin Pierre!' shouted Sharkadder. 'Over here! It's me, Sharkadder! He's my cousin, you know,' she informed everyone importantly.

'And now, O ladies and gentlemen, put your hands together for your own, your very own Mr Dunfer Malpractiss, local shopkeeper!' announced Ali Pali, to a chorus of jeers. 'Chosen because of his winning ways and the fact that in the last month he has sold an astonishing *one thousand cans* of Reeka Reeka Roses! Congratulations, Dunfer! See me afterwards.'

'I 'ope this won't take long,' grumbled Dunfer Malpractiss. 'I gorra get back to the shop.'

'And last of all,' said Ali Pali, 'we have last year's winner, Fumbling Phil and his Fantastic Feathered Friends.'

'Boooooo!' screamed the audience as a mild little

man in a heaving cardigan got to his feet and
bowed. 'Boooo! Loada rubbish! Ought never to
have got it! Booo!'

'All right, simmer down, simmer down. Well,
that's the introductions over, apart from saying a big
thank you to the Yeti Brothers for doing the bar
snacks and also the Witchway Rhythm Boys, here
to provide the drum-rolls and suchlike.'

A little burst of tuneless music came from the
orchestra pit, followed by a nasty thud as the drum-
mer dropped his stick.

'Be better off providin' the sausage rolls!' shouted
the heckling Fiend, and was rewarded by a few
appreciative titters.

'And now,' proclaimed the Master of Ceremonies,
'Now for the moment you've all been waiting for.
Time to get down to the real business of the evening
– the Spells!'

Ali Pali snapped his fingers and a small blue metal
waste-bin appeared at his feet. It appeared to be full
of folded scraps of paper.

'In time-honoured fashion, the running order will
be decided by picking names out of the bin. Right,
here goes. The first entry for the Spell of the Year
Competition is Scurfgo, the Celebrated Miracle
Anti-dandruff Shampoo, entered by Witch
Scrofula.'

A general sigh went up.

'Oh no, not again!'

'Seen it! Seen it!'

'Every year it's the same! Honestly, you'd think she'd at least change the name or something . . .'

Scrofula shot from her seat and flounced determinedly up to the stage with a foaming bucket in her hand. She always entered her Celebrated Shampoo and made the Judging Panel try and guess which side of her head had been washed in ordinary soap and which had been treated with the special stuff in the bucket. The Judges never, ever knew. Scrofula always retired hurt. It was all very boring and predictable.

In fact if one was honest, the Spell of the Year Competition as a whole was getting boring and predictable. Every year, the same old spells got dragged out and dusted off, maybe given a new name, but essentially the same as last year's offering.

After the Judging Panel had cast a hasty eye over Scrofula's hair, failed as always to spot the difference and sent the tearful failure scurrying back to cry on Barry's shoulder with a total of zero points, it was the turn of a Wizard.

'The next entry is Frank the Foreteller's Astonishing Oracle Tea-bag, without which no soothsayer's kit is complete,' announced Ali Pali.

The audience sat up a little and took a bit more notice. An Oracle Tea-bag didn't sound exactly earth-shattering, but at least it was new.

To Wizardly cheers, Frank the Foreteller strolled on-stage and gave a knowing smirk. From one sleeve he produced a kettle and from the other, a cup and saucer. Then from under his hat, he produced a small square tea-bag, which he held carefully between thumb and forefinger.

'Ladies and Gentlemen, I will now demonstrate this remarkable new fortune-telling Oracle Tea-bag,' said Frank the Foreteller. 'This tea-bag is the *only one* of its kind! This tea-bag is quick, reliable, and saves all those messy tea-leaves. And you can use it again and again. Could I have a volunteer, please?'

Quick as a flash, a small, furry Thing wearing a Moonmad T-shirt was on the stage, hopping about excitedly and waving to its cheering friends in the back row.

'Right, sir, if you'd just like to stand to one side while I concentrate my amazing powers on boiling this kettle,' said Frank the Foreteller, shutting his eyes, holding his breath and going bright red. After a moment or two, steam poured from the spout and the kettle gave a shrill whistle.

The Wizard contingent clapped heartily in the hopes that this would influence the Judges. The rival Witches put in a bit of ostentatious yawning, and several members of the general public really did drop off to sleep.

'Huh. I could do that before I could walk,' remarked Pongwiffy. 'This is really dull. I wish it was our turn next.'

'It won't be,' said Sharkadder. 'I bet we have to sit through loads of rubbish before it's us. Sludgegooey's Wart Cream, Gaga's Motorized Rotating Bat Rack, Macabre's Sporran of Invisibility, Ratsnappy's Handy Pocket Wand Set, Greymatter's Dictionary of Useful Magical Terms . . .'

'Stop! Stop!' begged Pongwiffy. 'It's all the same as last year!'

'. . . and that's just us Witches,' finished Sharkadder. 'The Wizards'll be dredging up loads of dreary old stuff, if this act's anything to go by, and so will the rest of 'em. I wouldn't mind betting we'll be last on. I've got that feeling in my bones.'

'Well, I'm not sitting around watching. It's

making me nervous. Shall I get us all an ice-cream? There's a bar at the back.'

'Oh, yes please, Pong,' said Sharkadder, surprised. 'That would be lovely. Thank you.'

'The only thing is, I haven't got my purse,' said Pongwiffy sadly.

Sharkadder gave an exasperated sigh.

'Go on, then,' she said. 'Take my handbag. And make sure you check the change. And don't go getting anything too expensive. It's my money, remember.'

'All right. What d'you want?'

'A Bogberry lolly,' said Sharkadder.

'What does Dudley want?'

A growled response from somewhere under Sharkadder's chair indicated that Dudley wanted a Mouse 'n' Vanilla cornet.

'What about you, Hugo?'

Hugo didn't care as long as it had nuts.

CHAPTER TWENTY
AN ENCOUNTER AT

At the very back of the hall, on a rickety bench, behind a pillar, miles from the stage and in a freezing draught, sat the Goblins. Being Goblins, they had automatically been given the worst seats in the house. Unfair, yes – but for Goblins, life is.

Plugugly sat on the far left. Then came Slop-bucket, Eyesore, Stinkwart, Hog, Sproggit and Lardo. They sat with blank, uncomprehending faces, jaws drooping, hands frequently scratching their cropped heads, eyes fixed on the distant stage, watching Frank the Foreteller go through his paces.

Frank the Foreteller had now made his cup of tea, and was explaining to the Thing in the Moonmad T-shirt that the mystic art of tea-bag reading relied on the accurate, mathematical counting of the exact

number of wrinkles in the tea-bag and the scientific way it lay in the bottom of the cup, etc.

'Wassee on about?' Plugugly wanted to know.

'Beats me,' said Hog wonderingly. 'Makin' tea, ain't ee?'

'Probably the interval,' said Sproggit knowledgeably. 'You gets tea in the interval, see.'

(Young Sproggit had once helped shift scenery for the Skeleton production of *Rose Marie*, and considered himself to be an expert on all matters concerning the Boards.)

'Nah, s'not the interval,' disagreed Hog. 'Issa spell, innit? Ee's makin' a spell. Spellerdee Year, innit?'

'Whatever it is, iss rubbish,' observed Plugugly.

The Spell of the Year Competition wasn't for Goblins. Goblins couldn't understand all this Magic business. All those long words and all that finger-wiggling was far too complicated for them. In fact, they had only come in because:

1. It was raining outside.

2. Young Sproggit thought there might be refreshments in the interval.

'Now wassee doin'?' asked Plugugly.

Frank the Foreteller was carefully handing the steaming cup to the Thing in the Moonmad T-shirt, with instructions to sip slowly. The Thing, who had been nodding solemnly throughout, suddenly lost patience, snatched the cup, fished out the Amazing Oracle Tea-bag with hairy fingers and, much to the horror of Frank the Foreteller and the delight of everyone else, swallowed it in one. With one accord, the Judging Panel displayed seven more zeros.

And that was something else Frank the Foreteller failed to predict.

'Rubbish,' repeated Plugugly firmly.

'Lardo's cryin' again,' announced young Sproggit with relish. The other Goblins looked hopefully along the bench. Sure enough, huge tears were welling up in Lardo's eyes, brimming over and splashing down his cheeks. Slowly, unconsciously, his hand crept for the thousandth time to his head and searched in vain for his missing bobble.

''Ee's in mournin' fer 'is bobble,' jeered Slop-bucket, and the rest of the Goblins collapsed at the sheer subtlety of the humour. This was more like it. This was something they could understand. You could keep your old spells. A nice bit of spiteful teasing, now *that's* what you called entertainment.

'I's not,' protested Lardo, snatching his hand

down. 'I's got a runny eye cos I gotta cold. An' I's gotta sore throat too. I's fed up with this old Speller the Year. I's gonna buy a drink. Oo else wants one?'

'Me! Me! I do!' cried all the Goblins, eagerly shooting their hands in the air.

'Well 'ard luck, get yer own!' retorted Lardo with an air of triumph, and stood up. Plugugly being at the other end, the bench shot up and deposited all the Goblins on the floor.

'Serves you right,' chortled Lardo, pleased with his little witticism. Blowing his nose, he made his way around the back of the hall to the bar. He cast his eye over the audience, and thought he caught a glimpse of that Tree Demon, the one with the knives who had made him take his hat off before subjecting him to a humiliating short back and sides. And then his bobble got stolen and . . . Lardo shivered and hurried on to the bar.

A burly Yeti in a grease-stained red waistcoat and gold medallion was leaning on the counter, idly watching the far stage where Witch Gaga was demonstrating her Rotating Bat Rack. In the background, another identical Yeti in a floral pinny was chopping tomatoes with huge, curly paws. (These were the Yeti Brothers: Spag Yeti and Conf Yeti – Pasta and Weddings a Speciality.)

A couple of Skeletons were propped at the bar,

sipping long drinks through straws and sharing a packet of crisps. They looked up as Lardo approached and haughtily turned their backbones on him.

'Yeah? Whata ya wanna?' said the waistcoated Yeti (Spag).

'Demonade, please,' said Lardo.

'You Gobleena?' asked the Yeti.

'Eh?' asked Lardo, playing for time.

'I aska you Gobleena? Cosa we dona serva no Gobleena. You Gobleena?'

Lardo thought hard. Then, suddenly, in a flash, the right answer came to him. It was clever, it was cunning, and it just might work. 'No,' he said.

'Datsa OK den,' said Spag. 'Justa checkin'. No 'fensa. Demonada, huh? I getta froma de back, OK?'

'Fine,' said Lardo happily. 'Take your time. I'll just wait here.'

Congratulating himself on his clever little bit of subterfuge, he leaned casually on the bar and half turned to watch the stage, where Gaga's Rotating Bat Rack was spinning wildly out of control and showering the audience with dizzy bats.

It was at this point that Lardo saw Pongwiffy wending her way towards him up the aisle. She was holding a large black handbag which Lardo didn't recognize as hers. 'I bet you stole that handbag, Pongwiffy,' said Lardo as she came up. Just as a pleasant opening conversational remark.

'Go boil your bobble, Lardo,' retorted Pongwiffy, elbowing past him to the bar. 'Awful haircut, by the way,' she added unkindly.

Lardo desperately tried to think of a fitting insult, but for the life of him he couldn't. Playing that little joke on his fellow Goblins and all that quick-witted repartee with the barman had exhausted him creatively. So he resorted to what he always said in these circumstances. 'Ah shut up,' he said. Feeble, but the best he could do.

'By the way,' said Pongwiffy, standing on his foot. 'Where *is* your disgusting bobble? Didn't it used to live on the top of your horrible hat?'

Tears welled up in Lardo's eyes. He couldn't bear talking about his bobble.

'Someone took it,' he said.

'Is that so? Now, why in the world would anyone do that? Unless, of course, they intended to chop it up and use it in a spell, ha ha. Hey! Conf! Let's have some service here! One small Mouse 'n' Vanilla cone, one stingy-sized Bogberry lolly, something small and cheap with nuts for Hugo and an Extra-special-Double-scoop-Mega-chocko-Jammy-Surprise with Extra-rich Cherry Sauce and Double Cream for me.'

'Letsa see your money firsta, Pongwiffy,' said the tomato-chopper, not even bothering to look round. 'An' I donna meana dat Magic coin what always go backa to your pursa neither.'

'I don't know, the service these days,' grumbled Pongwiffy, scrabbling in the cavernous depths of Sharkadder's handbag. 'Oh bother, I can't find her purse. And I can't see a thing in this light. Hang on.'

And without more ado, she emptied the contents

of Sharkadder's handbag on to the counter. Combs, brushes, mirrors, tweezers, files, pliers, tubes of lipstick, pots of powder and about a thousand hair-grips spilt everywhere. Several tiny, surprised-looking hedgehogs poked their heads out of a frilly sponge-bag, climbed out and trotted away. In the midst of the clutter lay Sharkadder's purse.

And, of course, the small green demonade bottle containing the precious Wishing Water.

'Ah!' cried Pongwiffy, seizing upon the purse. 'Here it is. I knew it was in there somewhere. Look, see? I've got loads of money. So I want a small Mouse 'n' Vanilla, a stingy . . .'

'Your drinka, *Signor*. Sorry to keepa you waiting,' said the Yeti in the red waistcoat, returning to the counter with Lardo's drink.

Now, all this time, Lardo had been thinking. Pongwiffy's casual little remark about chopping up his bobble had set him off on a train of thought. It was the sort of train that went very slowly, stopped frequently and invariably arrived late. But it got there in the end.

''Ere,' said Lardo. 'Wachoo mean about my bobble . . .?'

But he never found out. At exactly that moment, there came an announcement from the stage.

'Ladies and Gentlemen, Witch Gaga's Rotating Bat Rack has been disqualified on safety grounds. So, without more ado we shall move on to the next act, which is a highly secret double entry from Pongwiffy and Sharkadder. Could we have the contestants on stage, please?'

'It's us!' gasped Pongwiffy in a panic. 'Oh bother, why didn't anyone tell me we were next? Wait for me! I'm coming, I'm coming!'

Unceremoniously, she scooped Sharkadder's junk back into her handbag, snatched up the precious bottle of Wishing Water and scuttled back down the aisle. Several legs stuck out to trip her up, but she cunningly avoided them.

She met up with Sharkadder at the foot of the stage. Sharkadder was suffering from first-night nerves, pacing anxiously up and down with her back to the audience, gnawing on her six-inch finger-nails.

'Oh, Pong, where have you *been*? It's our *turn*. Have you got the Wishing Water?'

'Yes, yes, of course I have. What d'you take me for? Come on, let's get on stage. The audience are getting restless.'

Indeed, the audience was starting a slow handclap, and a group of Banshees in the back row had set up a shrill, impatient screaming. Scrofula and Barry were encouraging some synchronized booing and Agglebag and Bagaggle had come up with a nice line in hissing. Right now, Pongwiffy wasn't the most popular name on everyone's lips.

'Wait a minute, wait a minute, I need my lipstick. I want to look my best for my public. Oh my badness! Whatever have you done to my handbag?'

'Never mind that now!' shouted Pongwiffy crossly. 'It's all your fault anyway! You were so sure we wouldn't be on till last. You felt it in your bones, you said.'

'Oh, do stop going on! There. I've done my lips. Now, just give me the Wishing Water, and we'll get on stage.'

'What d'you mean, give *you* the Wishing Water? If anyone's carrying the Wishing Water it's me. It's my spell. I found the recipe.'

'Oh the cheek of it! Who helped you make the

brew? Who baked you a sponge when all your other so-called friends deserted you? Eh?'

'Having problems, ladies?' inquired the silky tones of Ali Pali from the stage.

'Certainly not,' snapped Pongwiffy. 'Stand back, Pali, and prepare to be amazed. Me and my assistant are coming up.'

And up they went.

CHAPTER TWENTY-ONE

Wishing Water

'All right, you lot, simmer down! Get lost, Pali, I can do my own announcements thanks very much. Ladies and Gentlemen, I have here, in this perfectly ordinary small green demonade bottle, the most won –'

'What did you mean, "my assistant"?' inquired Sharkadder.

'Eh? Oh, shush, Sharky, now's not the time to get on your high horse. Ahem. As I was saying, Ladies and Gentlemen . . .'

'No, I'm sorry, but I'd like to get this clear from the start. What exactly did you mean by "my assistant"?'

Pongwiffy's brain spun madly. If Sharkadder took umbrage now, everything could be ruined. Luckily, inspiration came.

'Because you're the beautiful one, of course. Haven't you ever noticed? Conjuror's assistants are always very glamorous and dressed in lovely clothes and things. Like you.'

'Oh. Oh, I see what you mean. Yes, I suppose

you're right,' admitted Sharkadder, tossing her hair and treating the riotous audience to a sudden, dazzling smile.

'So, can I get on with what I was saying?'

'Yes. Yes, of course,' purred Sharkadder, placing a hand on a hip and striking the sort of showy pose she imagined a conjuror's glamorous assistant might strike.

'Good. Ladies and Gentlemen, as I was saying, before you, in this humble little bottle, you see the winning potion of this year's Spell of the Year Competition. For this little bottle contains a sample of none other than the legendary Wishing Water, made to Granny Malodour's very own recipe!'

There was a surprised pause, followed by some excited whispering and a fair amount of disbelieving laughter. Granny Malodour's famous Wishing Water, eh? A likely story. Why, everyone knew that the recipe had been lost in the mists of time.

'Go ahead, laugh!' Pongwiffy told them.

'You'll be laughing on the other side of your faces in a minute. My lovely assistant Sharkadder will now offer each of the Judges a small amount of this amazing potion. A Wish each. That's what they get. And if their wishes don't come true, my lovely assistant will personally eat her pointy hat. Sharp end first. That's how confident I am of this spell.'

'Hang on there just a minute . . .' objected the lovely assistant. But Pongwiffy was in full swing, and there was no stopping her.

'Just to ensure there is no cheating, I will ask the Judges to write down a brief description of their Wish. Think carefully, now. This is the chance of a lifetime.'

The Judging Panel thought carefully. One Wish. The chance of a lifetime. They mustn't mess this up.

King Futtout II thought longingly of becoming a hermit and living in a cave on a mountain, far from the trappings of power; Scott Sinister dreamed of rave reviews of his latest film (*Revenge of the Killer Poodles*); Sourmuddle wished her memory was better, then forgot; the Venerable Harold the Hood-winker wished he was home in bed; Dunfer Mal-practiss had a fleeting vision of thousands of highly successful Malpractiss Magic Inc. Megastores strad-dling the globe and Pierre de Gingerbeard wished for the thousandth time that Sharkadder wasn't his cousin. Phil and his Feathered Friends didn't wish for anything, because they were in the gents at the time.

And then, as Pongwiffy instructed, the Judges (all except Phil) wrote their wishes down whilst Shark-adder poured out a few drops of the precious liquid in their water-glasses.

'Right,' said Pongwiffy after the pouring had been completed and the pieces of paper collected up. 'The wishes are as follows: Cave, Fame, Good Memory, Bed, Money, Not To Be Related To Sharkadder. Could we have a drum-roll, please? Silence, everyone. The Judges are about to sample the Wishing Water. Ready Judges? All together now . . . *Bottoms Up!*'

The Witchway Rhythm Boys played something vaguely tension-building and the audience held their breaths as the panel raised their glasses and drank. There was a long pause. Then:

'Tastes like demonade to me,' said Scott Sinister with a shrug.

'What?' said Pongwiffy. 'What did you say, Scott, dear?'

'I said it tastes like ordinary demonade. Don't you agree?' he asked his fellow Judges, who chorused their agreement.

'It's nothing like Granny's Wishing Water, Pongwiffy,' said Sourmuddle. 'And I can't remember what I wished for, but I'm pretty sure I haven't got it. Has anybody here got their wish?'

'No,' chimed in the judging panel. 'No we haven't! Boo!'

'I don't understand it,' wailed Pongwiffy, ringing her hands. 'What's happened? I made it to the exact recipe. It's got to be right. Surely *somebody* got their wish?'

Then it happened. Suddenly, without any warning, something soft and green plopped on her head. This was followed by another one, only this time it was blue. Then a tartan one. And then . . . *it began to rain bobbles*! Hundreds of them. Thousands of them. Millions and trillions and zillions of them. All different colours and different sizes. Big bright jolly yellow ones and pretty little pale-pink ones. Sensible navy ones and lurid multi-coloured ones. It was a bobble blizzard.

Softly fell the bobbles on to the heads and shoulders of the bewildered audience, rolling off and bouncing in the aisles, filling up the orchestra pit, settling in niches and corners, piling up in drifts against the exit doors. In seconds, everyone was ankle-deep in them – and still they kept coming.

'Don't panic! Stay calm!' instructed Ali Pali, before vanishing in a green puff.

People instantly panicked and made for the exits. King Futtout lost his crown, Sourmuddle's corns took a severe bashing, the trestle-table got overturned and somebody stole the silver cup. The tide of bobbles rose higher by the second, and several Dwarfs and small Gnomes were already waist-deep and struggling.

Never-ending bobbles. Raining down. Filling up the world.

Now, whoever could have wished for that?

CHAPTER TWENTY-TWO

A LOVELY SURPRISE

'Well it wasn't my fault,' muttered Pongwiffy for the umpteenth time.

'Yes it was,' argued Sharkadder. 'Everyone says so, don't they, Hugo? There won't be any Spell of the Year Competitions ever again, and it's all your fault. Why don't you admit it? Pass the frogs, please.'

It was the following day. They were sitting in Pongwiffy's unnaturally clean hovel. Sharkadder had brought over a tin of ginger frogs, and they were morosely dunking them in bogwater whilst raking over recent events in the hopes of finding someone to blame.

'You should have noticed it wasn't Wishing Water,' grumbled Pongwiffy. 'You should have noticed when you poured it out. Some assistant you turned out to be.'

'Oh yes? And who got the bottles muddled in the first place? Honestly, the ingratitude of it! That's the last time I lend you my handbag, Pongwiffy. And the last time I help you out with your rotten old spells.'

'Hugo should have noticed, then,' sulked Pongwiffy. 'What's the point of having a Familiar if he doesn't notice things?'

'I deed,' objected Hugo. 'I shout from ze stalls. I shout "Mistress, you got ze wrong bottle," I shout. But you no hear.'

There was a long pause. Then: 'It's the waste,' Pongwiffy said gloomily. 'That's what I can't get over. The waste of a perfectly good bottle of Wishing Water. And for what? So some stupid Goblin can have a lifetime's supply of bobbles. *Bobbles!* I ask you.'

'That's Goblins for you,' agreed Sharkadder.

'All that trouble, and I didn't even get to taste it.'

There was an even longer pause.

'I think I'm going to cry,' said Pongwiffy. And she did. Noisily, into a disgusting old hanky.

'Oh, cheer up, Pong, do,' said Sharkadder, giving her a little pat on the shoulder. 'It's not all bad. At least Ronald got his come-uppance. I hear he's got a shocking cold after I dunked him in the fountain.'

'And zat awful 'Unnydimple,' chimed in Hugo. 'Ve teach 'er lesson, uh?'

'And you've still got the recipe,' Sharkadder reminded her. 'You can always make some more.'

'What, after all the trouble I went to the first

time? Not likely. I nearly killed myself getting all those ingredients,' wept Pongwiffy. Adding: 'And nobody likes me any more.'

'I do,' said Sharkadder kindly.

'Me too,' said Hugo.

'No you don't. You were right. It was all my fault. It was all my fault that the audience stampeded and the cup got stolen and everything. It isn't surprising everyone hates me. I'm the most unpopular Witch in the Coven.'

'W-e-ll – yes,' admitted Sharkadder. 'Yes, you are. But that's nothing new. And you're still my best friend,' she added loyally.

'And mine,' nodded Hugo.

'Really? You mean it?' sniffed Pongwiffy.

'Certainly we do. And just to prove it, we've got something for you, haven't we, Hugo?'

Sharkadder reached for her handbag and took

something out. She handed it to Pongwiffy with an air of triumph.

'There. For you. It's the bottle of Wishing Water. Hugo took it off Lardo before he could finish it. We saved it for you. There's just enough drops left in there for a wish, I'd say.'

'He did? You did? There is? You mean, I'm going to sample Granny's Wishing Water after all?' Pongwiffy took the bottle with trembling fingers. 'But why didn't you tell me? Why wait till now?'

'We were waiting to hear you say it was all your fault,' explained Sharkadder. 'We wanted to see you grovel before springing this lovely surprise on you. Are you pleased?'

'Pleased? I'll say I'm pleased. Thanks, you two. Right, here goes. I'm going to make my wish. But first, Granny's Magic words . . . *Bottoms Up!*'

Eagerly, she raised the almost empty demonade bottle and drained it. Sharkadder and Hugo watched, eyes popping, as she lowered it and made a face.

'Yuck,' said Pongwiffy. 'Yep. That's Wishing Water all right. Pass me a ginger frog, Hugo. I need it to take the taste away.'

'Vat you vish for, Mistress?' asked Hugo eagerly.

'Wait. Be patient. You'll find out.'

They waited. And waited. Sharkadder was just about to remark that Wishing Water didn't appear

to be all that Pongwiffy cracked it up to be, when finally, something happened. A sudden wind blew up. At the same time, a low rumbling noise came from outside. There were crashings and slitherings, clankings and clatterings, tinklings and jinglings. There was also a very nasty smell in the air. The hovel door exploded open – and in flowed a mighty river of rubbish! It was like a dam bursting. Everything that Hugo and the Broom had worked so hard to get rid of came pouring back in, bringing with it a lot of extra dirt and debris that hadn't even been there in the first place.

Sharkadder shrieked, snatched up her skirts and leapt on the table for safety. Pongwiffy and Hugo hastily joined her, and all three of them huddled together and watched in amazement as the sea of trash slowly reclaimed the hovel.

All Pongwiffy's cast-offs were there – the old socks, the broken glasses, the bits of cheese, the maggot collection, the cauldron, the teddy, the hot-water bottle, the . . . well, you know. All of it.

After oozing around all over the floor for a bit, the rubbish began to separate out into recognizable bits. The various components made for their old, familiar nooks and crannies where they settled comfortably, obviously pleased to be back home again.

The old newspapers flapped their pages and flew clumsily up to a high shelf, where they formed themselves into untidy piles. The hot-water bottle gave a little leap and hung itself on a nail in the wall.

Sharkadder, Pongwiffy and Hugo ducked as crumbling old spell books with half the pages missing whizzed past their

ears and hurled themselves back into the bookcase any old how.

The sofa came crashing back in, broken springs waving jauntily and settled in its old place with a proprietorial air. Drawers slid open, waiting for the dozens of odd socks and old cardigans to crawl back into them. A disgracefully filthy sheet spread itself on the bed (over the nice clean one), tucked itself in (badly) and waited for its coating of biscuit crumbs to arrive.

All the pieces of broken, dirty china made for the sink, and soon the draining-board was piled high. While all this was going on, the window cracked and dirtied itself, cobwebs sneaked back over the ceiling and dust rained down in a steady shower.

Outside, weeds grew up the walls and all the fresh paint peeled off the door. At the same time, a party of starved-looking Spiders came wandering up the garden path crying, 'How about this, Ma. It looks even worse than the last place. Oh, my legs, it *is* the last place! How come?'

The Broom, aware that there was some sort of emergency, came whizzing in from outside, took one look at the state of the floor and promptly passed out.

When the dust had finally settled and the Spiders had unpacked and the last dead plant had finished arranging itself tastefully on the window-sill,

Sharkadder, Pongwiffy and Hugo slowly climbed down from the table.

'So,' said Sharkadder, tutting and looking around. 'This is your wish, is it, Pongwiffy? To live in squalor.'

'It certainly is,' said Pongwiffy, eyes glowing. 'It suits my personality, don't you think? I've been very unhappy these last two weeks. It just wasn't my own little hovel any more, not since it got spring-cleaned. I'm sorry, Hugo. After all your hard work.'

Hugo gave a little shrug.

'Ee's OK. After all, you vitch of dirty 'abits. I should know better. Besides, I sorta missed ze Spiders, you know?'

Up above, lots of little legs clapped together approvingly, and Gerald, the smallest Spider, took a dive into Hugo's bedside glass of water, out of sheer high spirits.